THE NO-GOOD DO-GOOD PIRATES

Jim Kraft   illustrated by Lynne Avril

www.av2books.com

Your AV² Media Enhanced book gives you a fiction readalong online. Log on to www.av2books.com and enter the unique book code from this page to use your readalong.

AV² Readalong Navigation

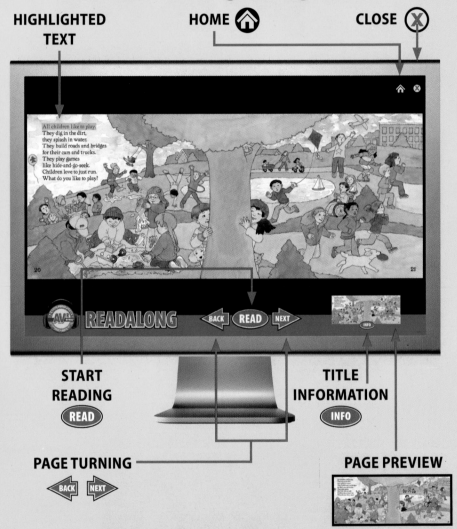

HIGHLIGHTED TEXT
HOME
CLOSE
All children like to play.
They dig in the dirt,
they splash in water.
They build roads and bridges
for their cars and trucks.
They play games
like hide-and-go-seek.
Children love to just run.
What do you like to play?
20
21
READALONG
BACK
READ
NEXT
INFO
START READING
READ
TITLE INFORMATION
INFO
PAGE TURNING
BACK
NEXT
PAGE PREVIEW

Go to **www.av2books.com,** and enter this book's unique code.

BOOK CODE

H391340

AV² by Weigl brings you media enhanced books that support active learning.

First Published by

ALBERT WHITMAN & COMPANY
Publishing children's books since 1919

Published by AV² by Weigl
350 5th Avenue, 59th Floor New York, NY 10118
Website: www.av2books.com www.weigl.com

Printed in the United States of America in North Mankato, Minnesota
1 2 3 4 5 6 7 8 9 0 17 16 15 14 13

052013
WEP250413

Library of Congress Control Number: 2013939934

ISBN 978-1-62127-896-2 (hardcover)
ISBN 978-1-48961-453-7 (single-user eBook)
ISBN 978-1-48961-454-4 (multi-user eBook)

For Jean, Jeff, and Matt. J.K.
To Forrest.—L.A.

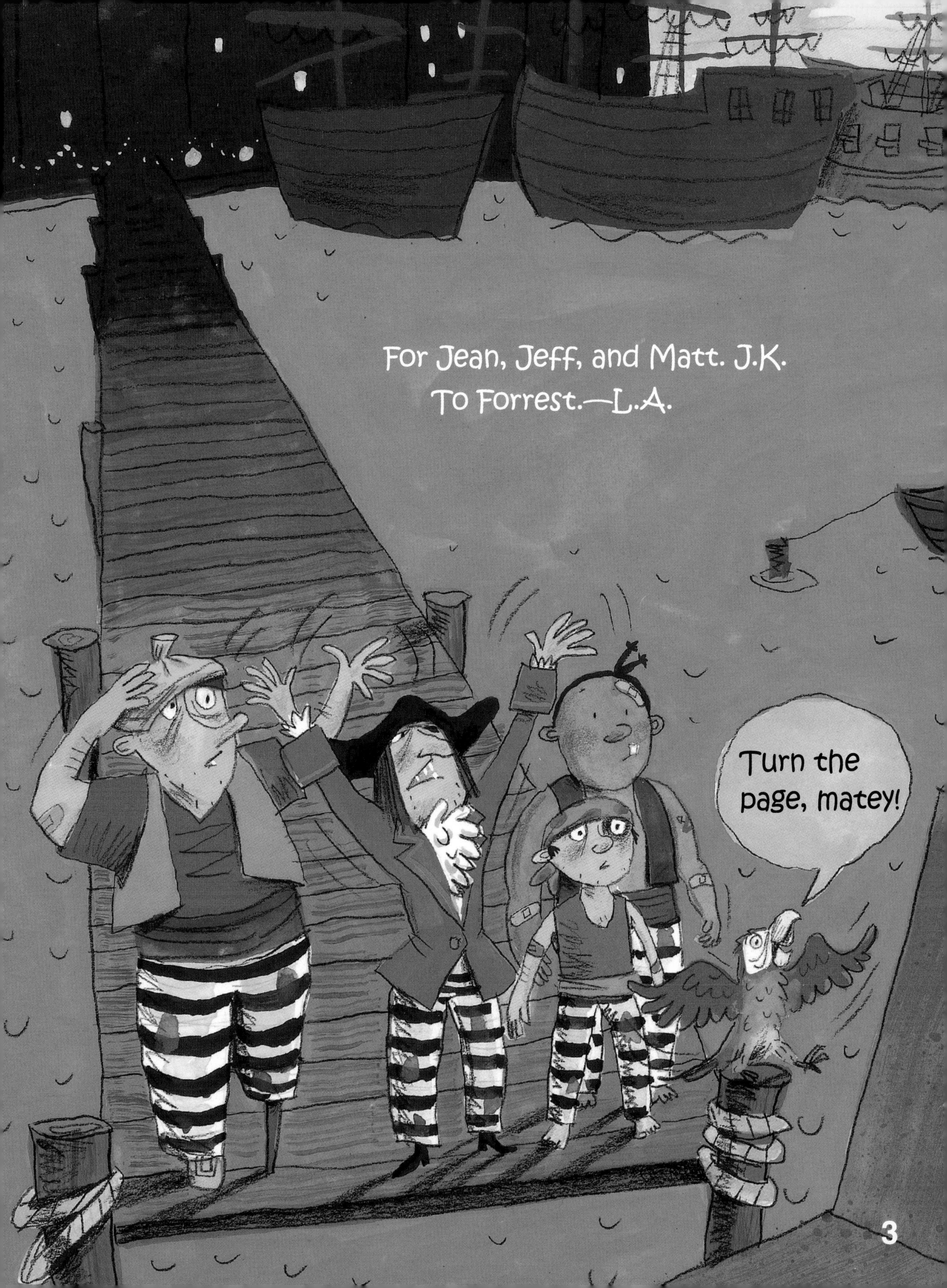
Turn the page, matey!

Here's a tale of four no-good pirates—Captain Squint, Ed the Fierce, One-Tooth Willy, and Smelly Bob. They prowled the seas in their ship, the *Flying Pig*.

These pirates were so bad . . .

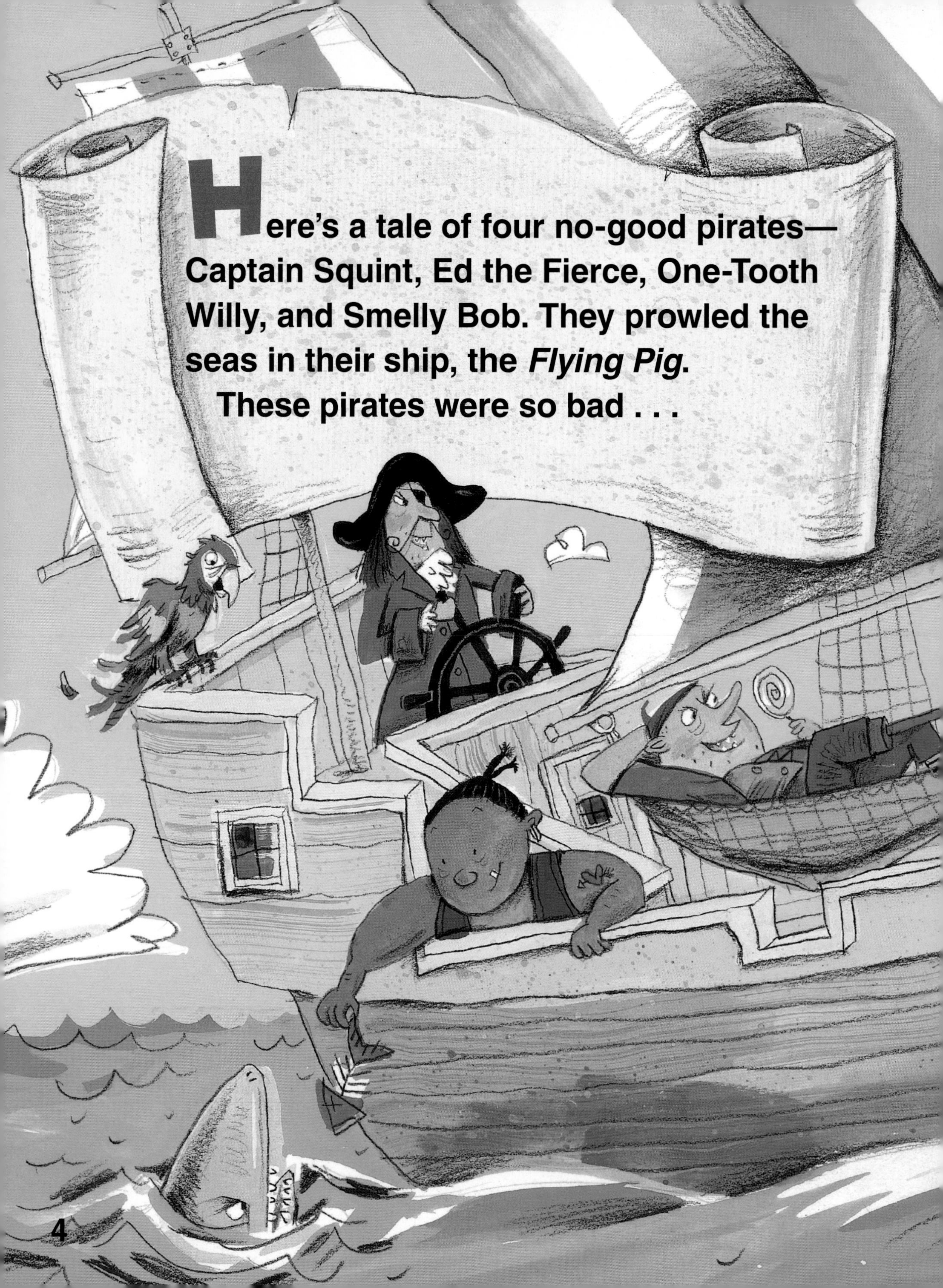

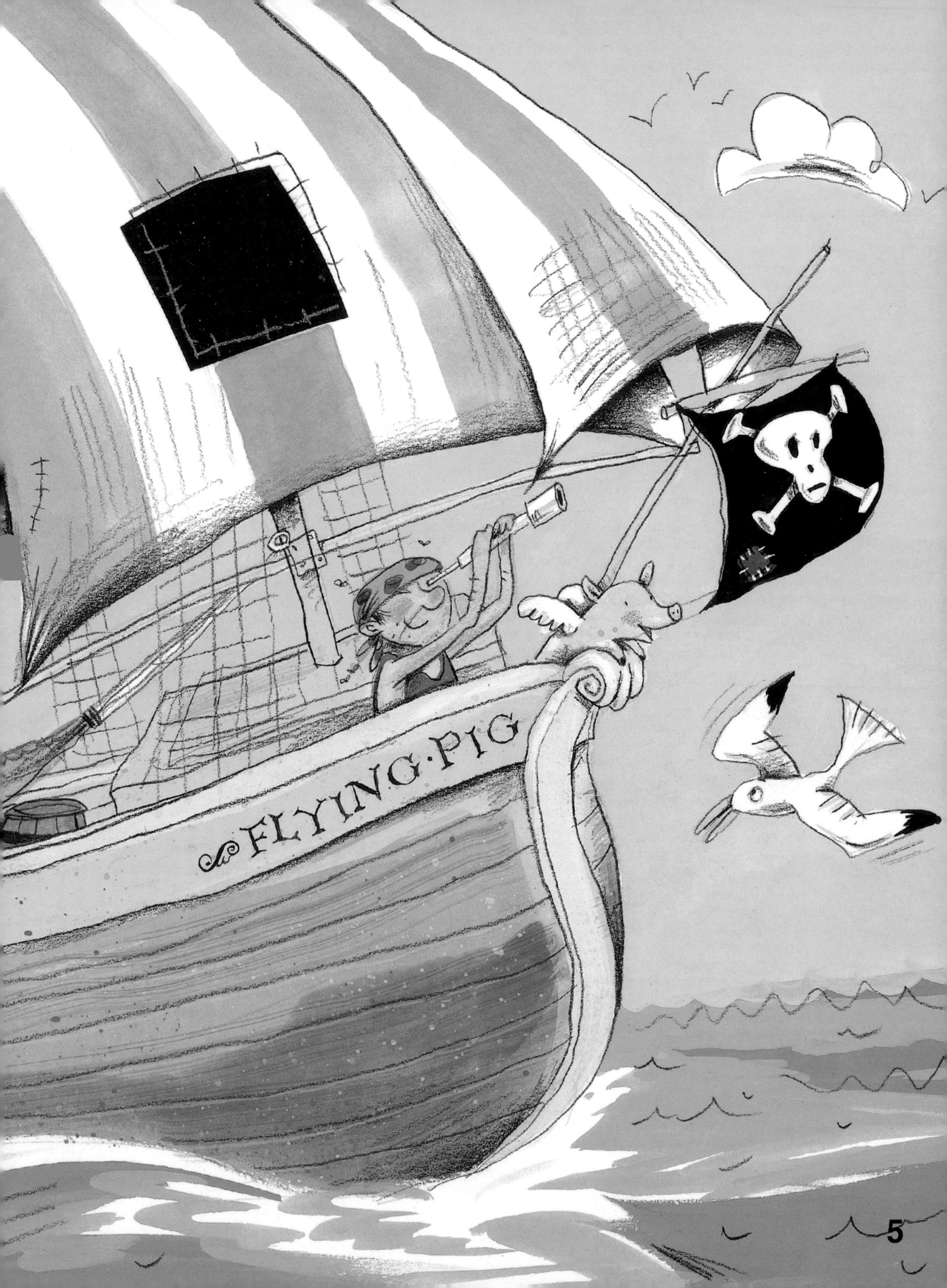
FLYING·PIG

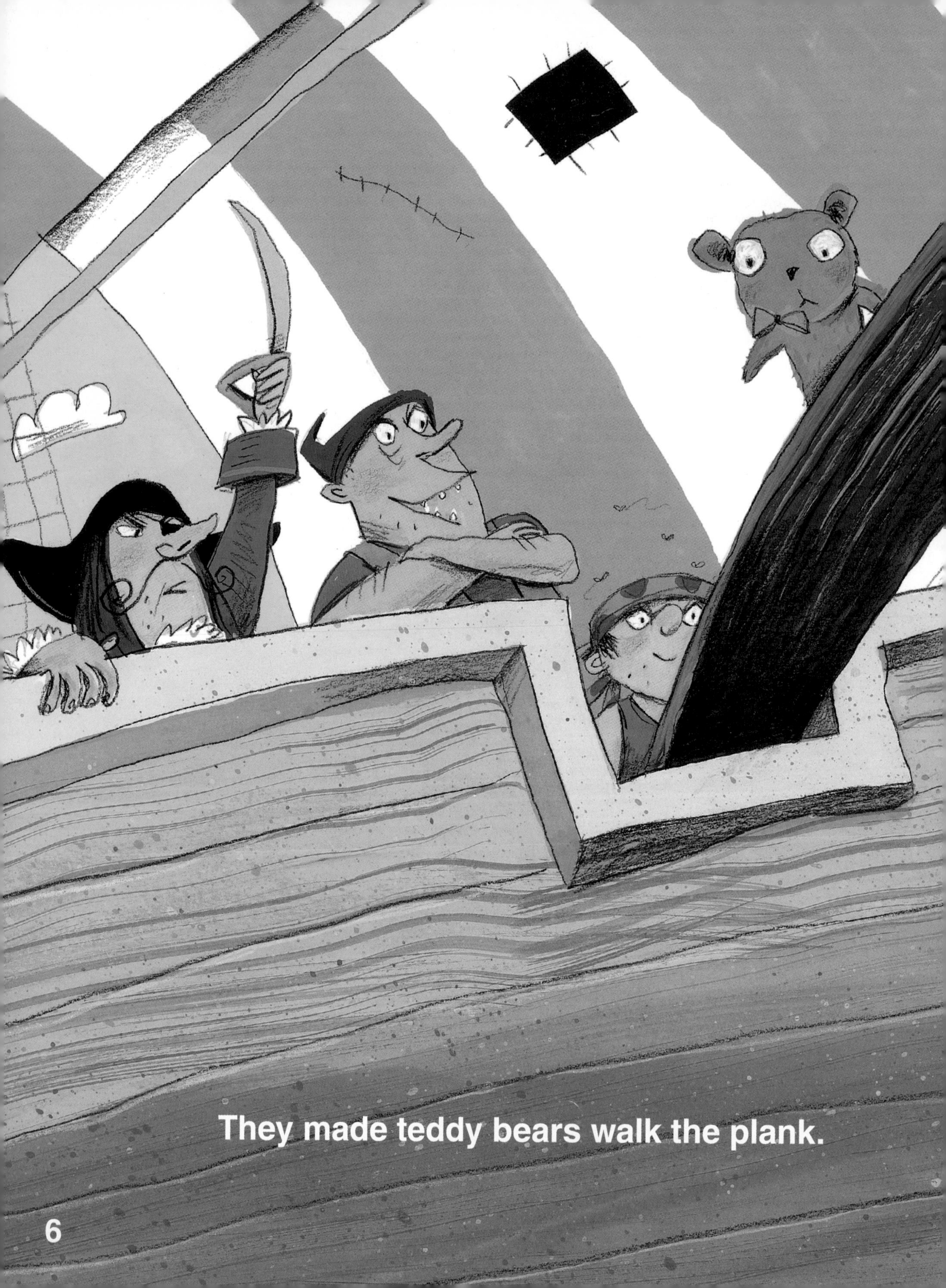

They made teddy bears walk the plank.

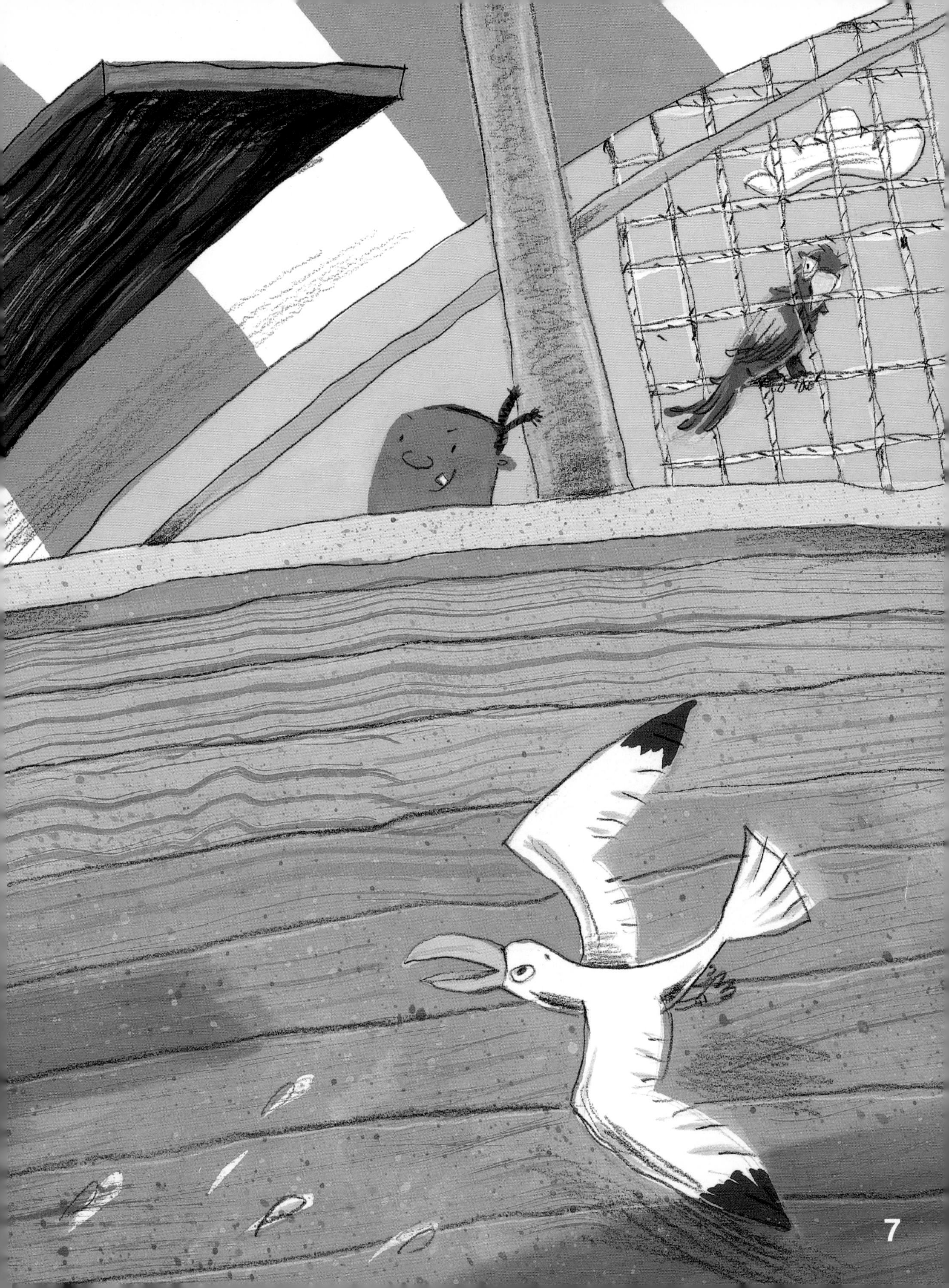

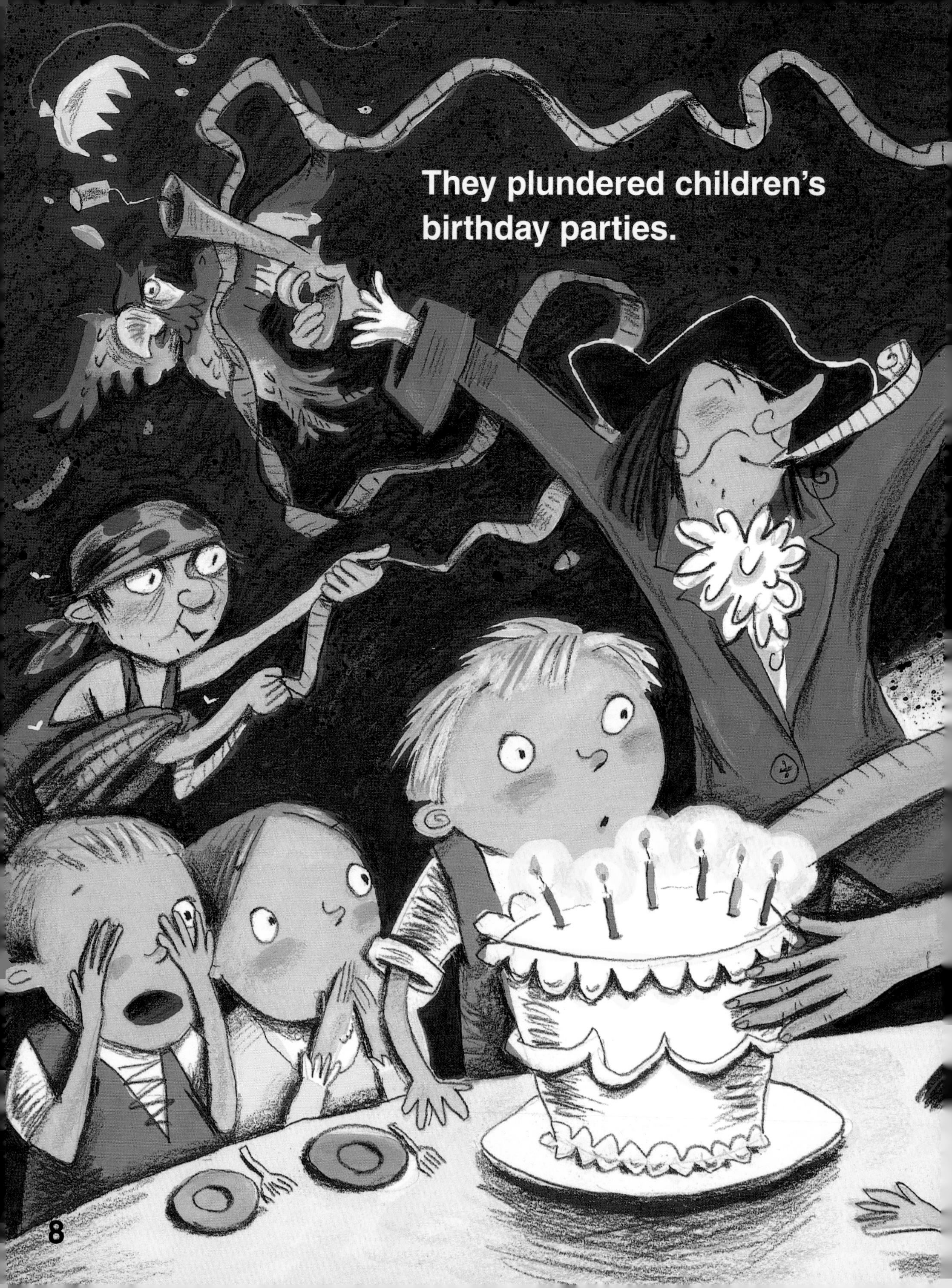

They plundered children's birthday parties.

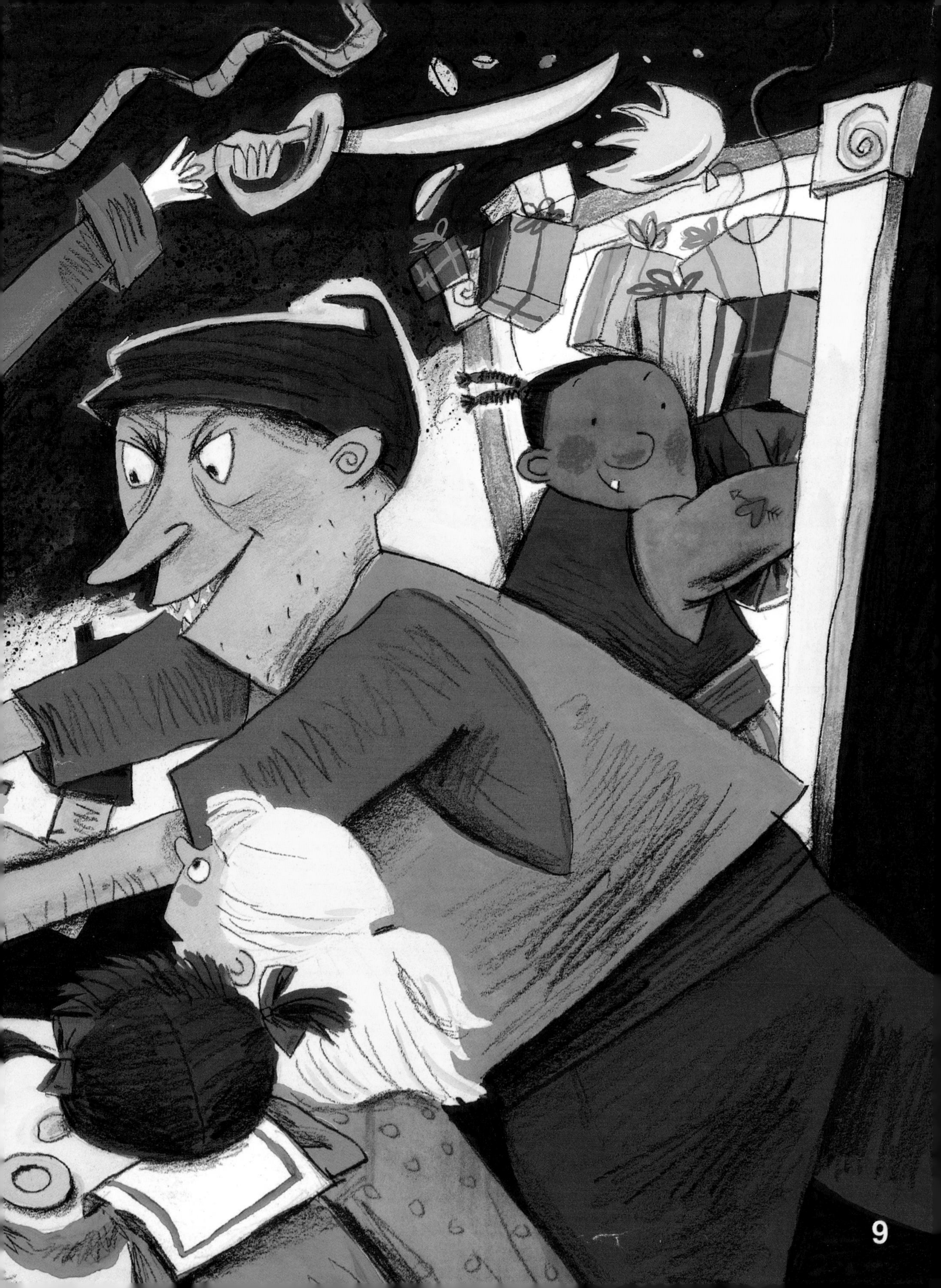

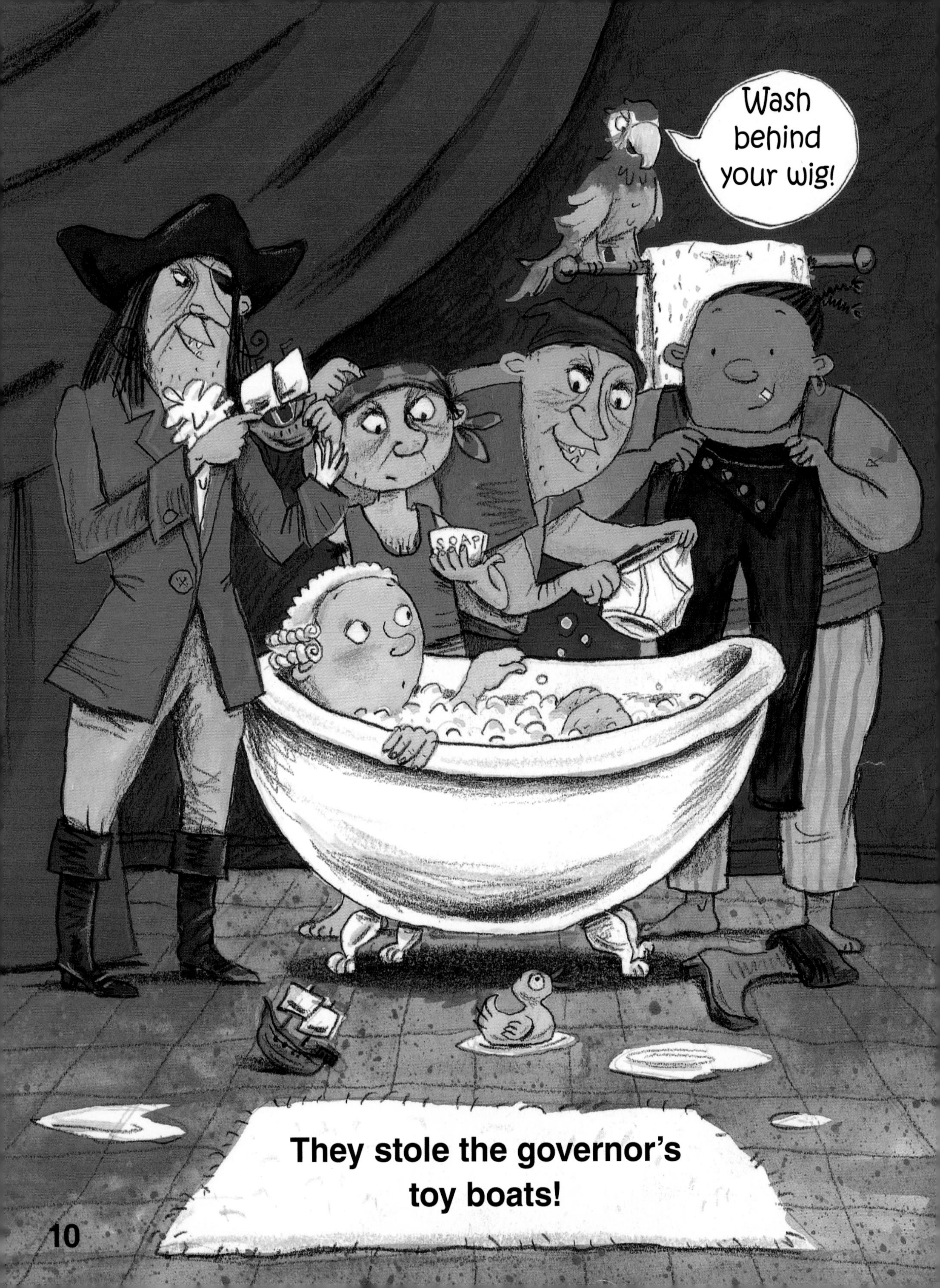
Wash behind your wig!
SOAP

They stole the governor's toy boats!

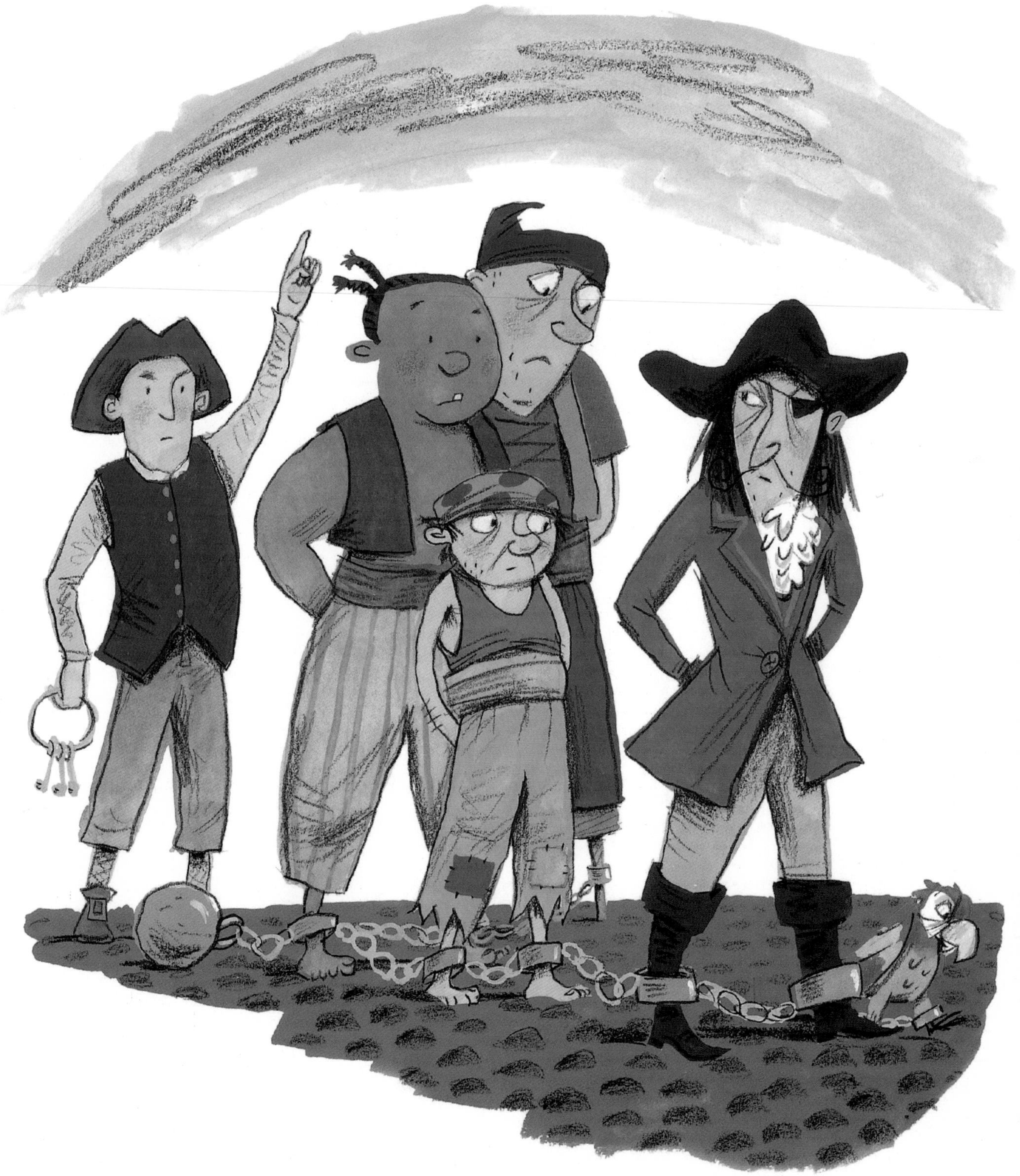

At last, these no-good pirates
were caught by the law.

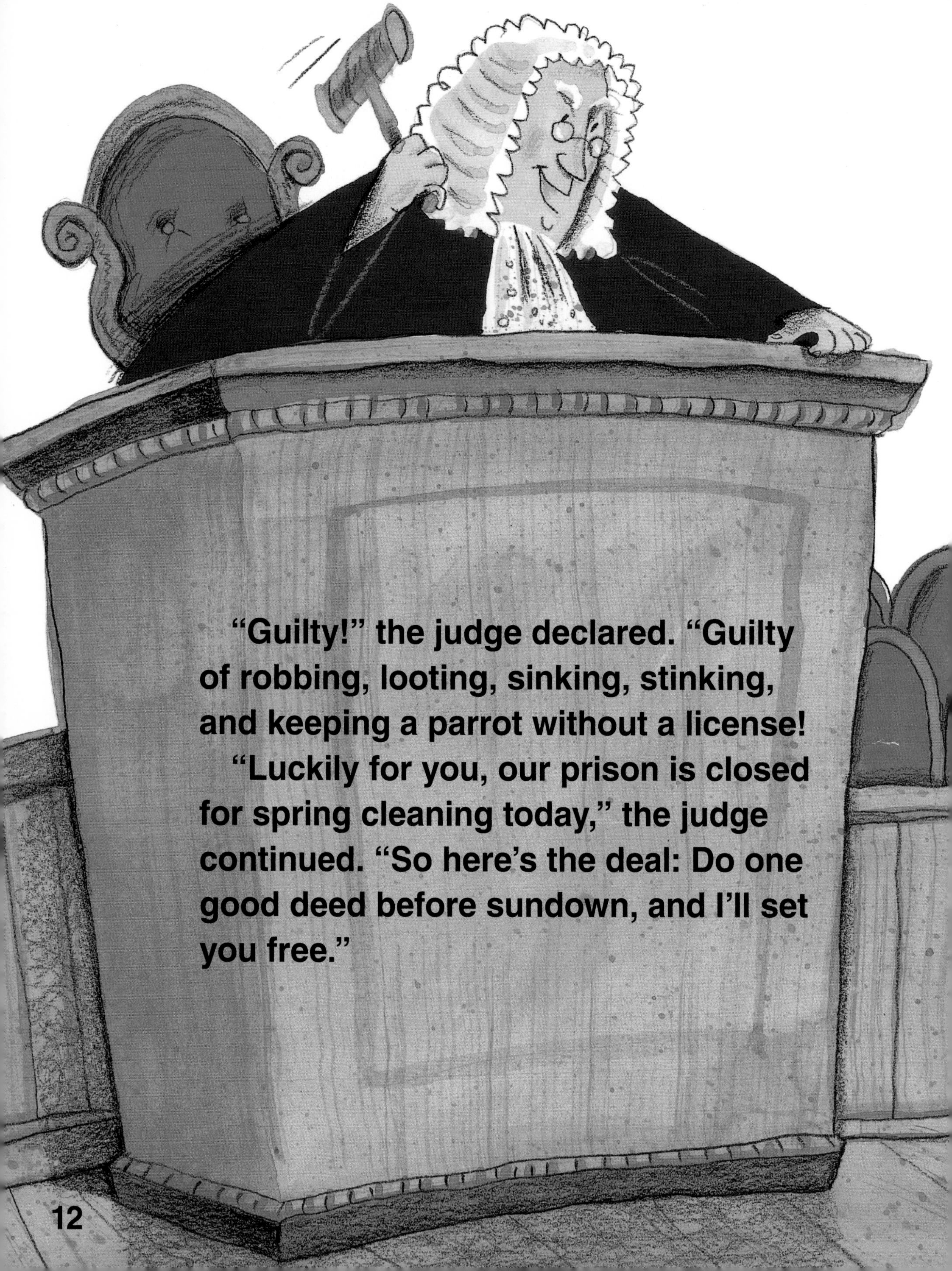

"Guilty!" the judge declared. "Guilty of robbing, looting, sinking, stinking, and keeping a parrot without a license!

"Luckily for you, our prison is closed for spring cleaning today," the judge continued. "So here's the deal: Do one good deed before sundown, and I'll set you free."

"What's a good deed?" Captain Squint whispered.
None of the pirates knew.

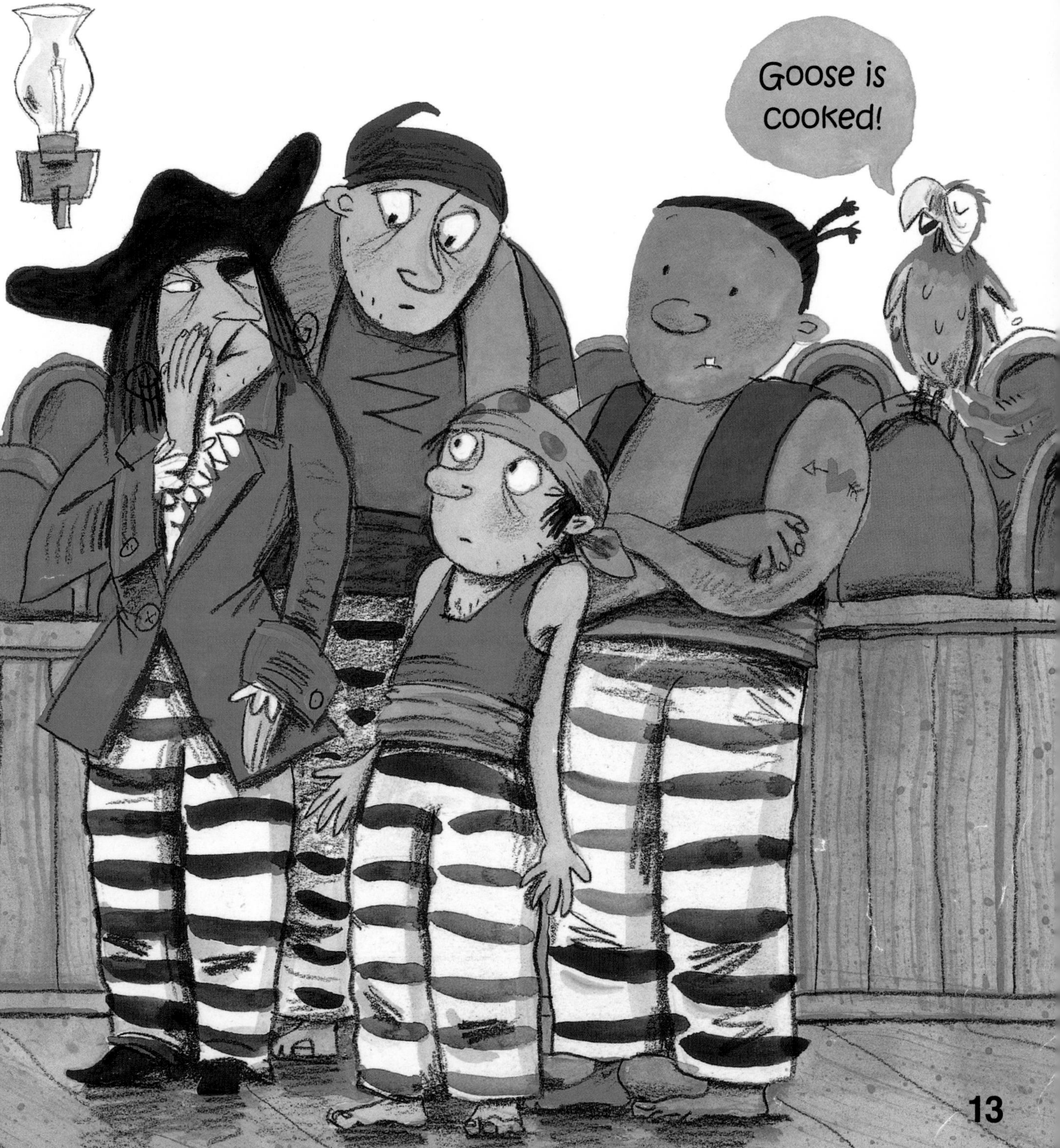
Goose is cooked!

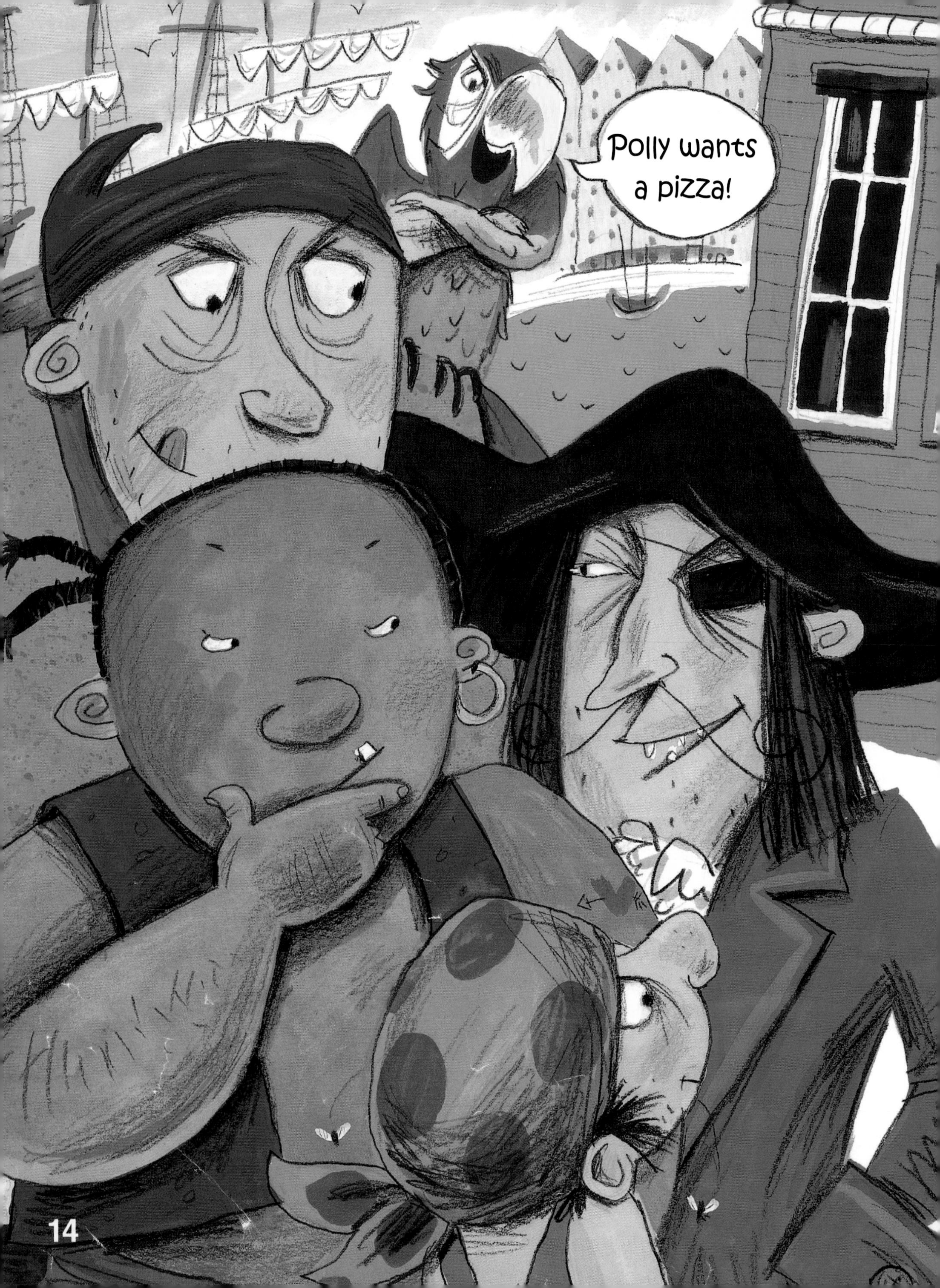
Polly wants a pizza!

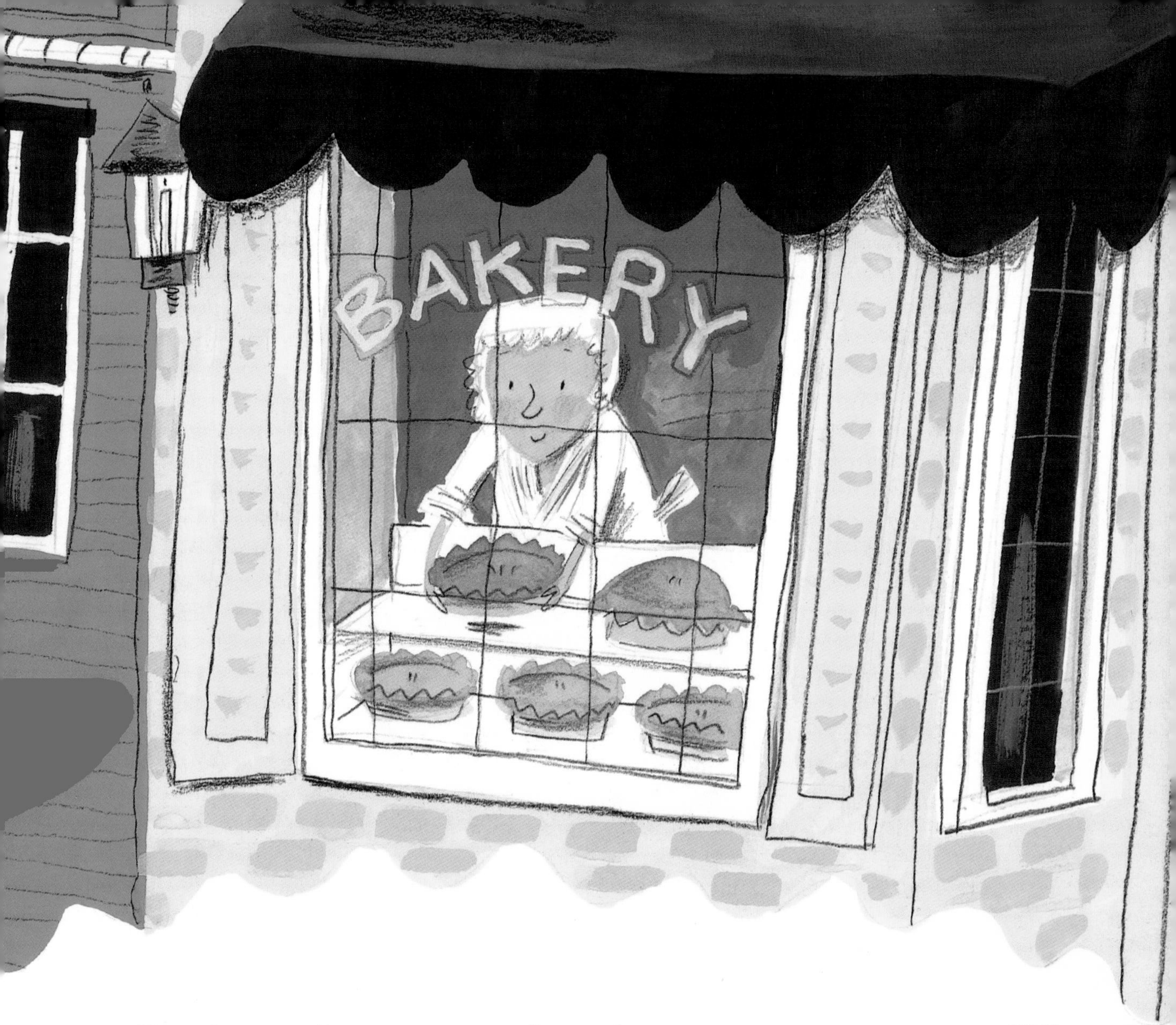
BAKERY

Back on the street, the pirates saw a woman filling a shop window with freshly baked pies.

"Suppose we was to eat all them pies," One-Tooth Willy suggested. "Then that lady could close the shop and snooze all afternoon. Wouldn't that be a good deed?"

"It sounds good to me!" Captain Squint declared. The pirates barged into the shop and began stuffing pies into their mouths.

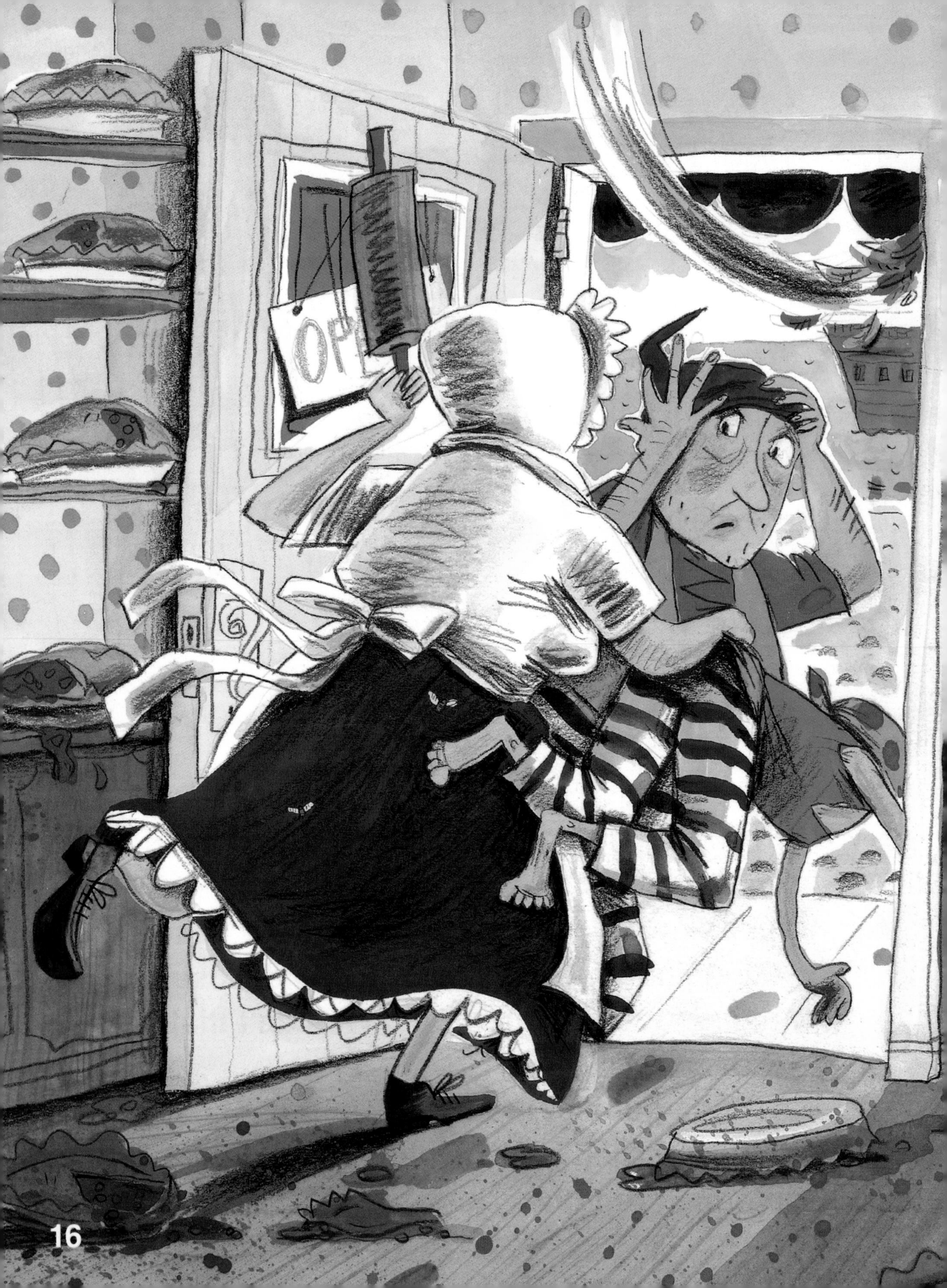
OPE

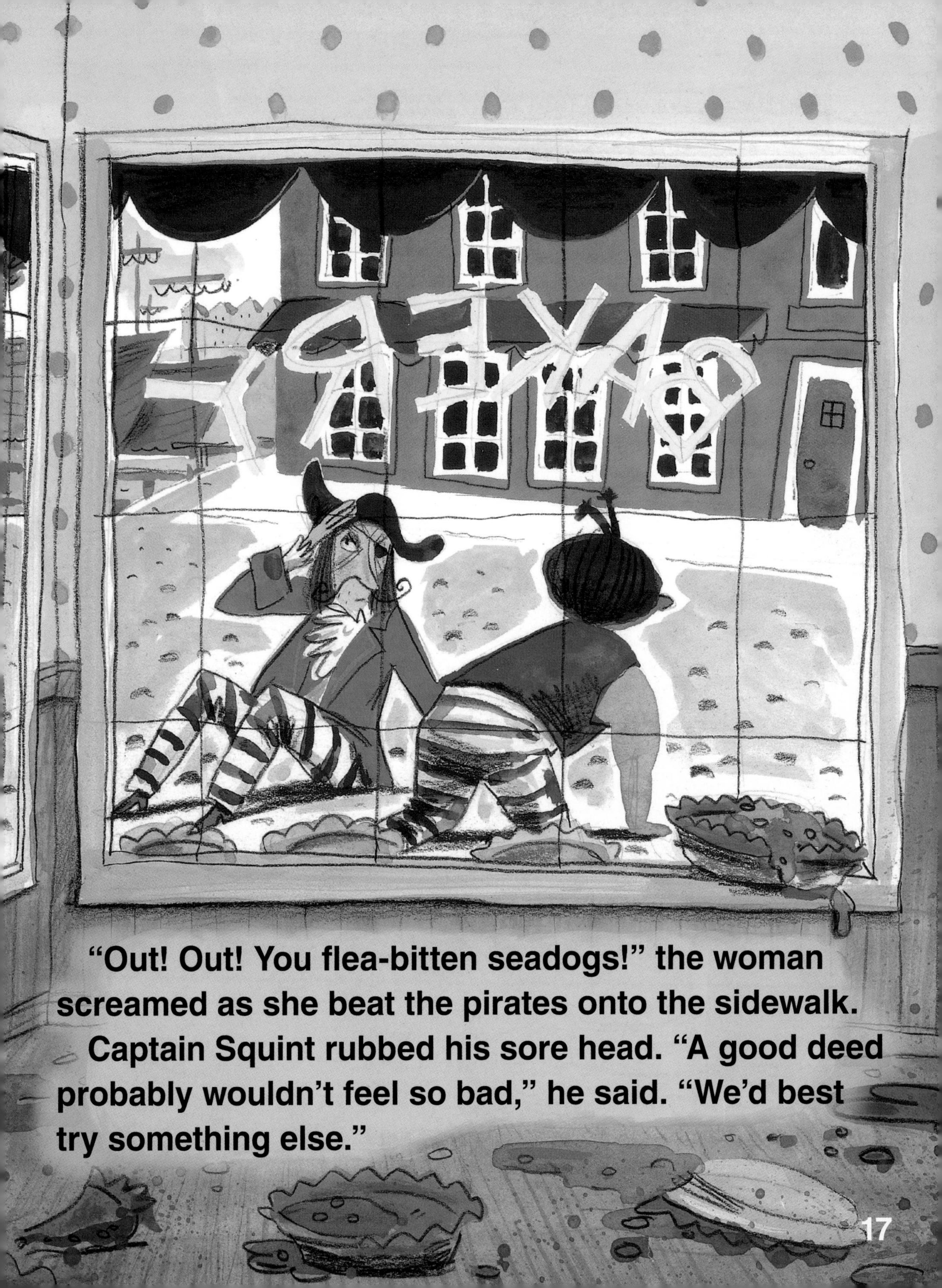

"Out! Out! You flea-bitten seadogs!" the woman screamed as she beat the pirates onto the sidewalk.

Captain Squint rubbed his sore head. "A good deed probably wouldn't feel so bad," he said. "We'd best try something else."

All day long, the pirates tried to do a good deed. At the bank, they thought it might be good to sweep the loose money into a sack. But the bank guards threw them out the door.

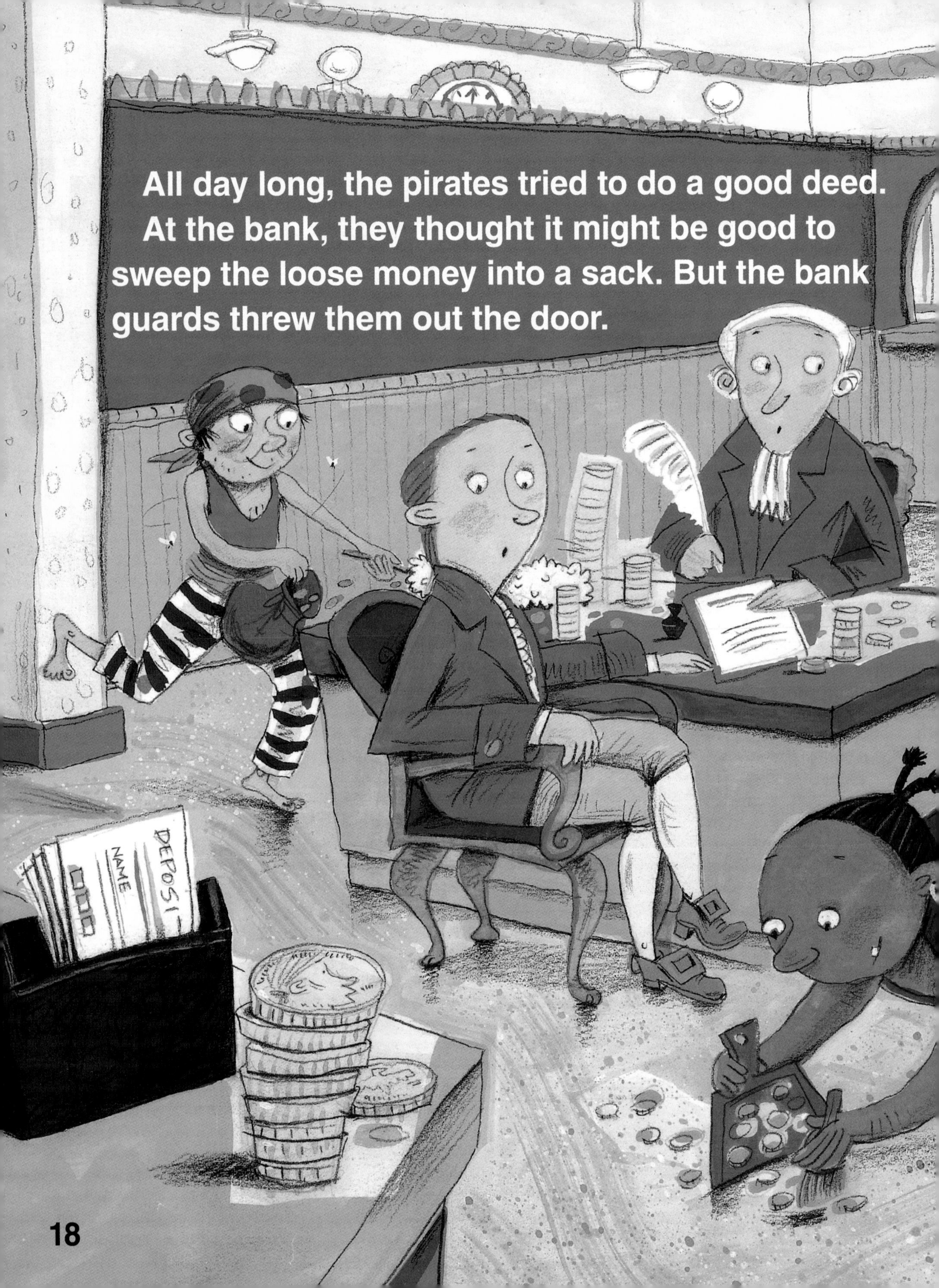
DEPOSI
NAME

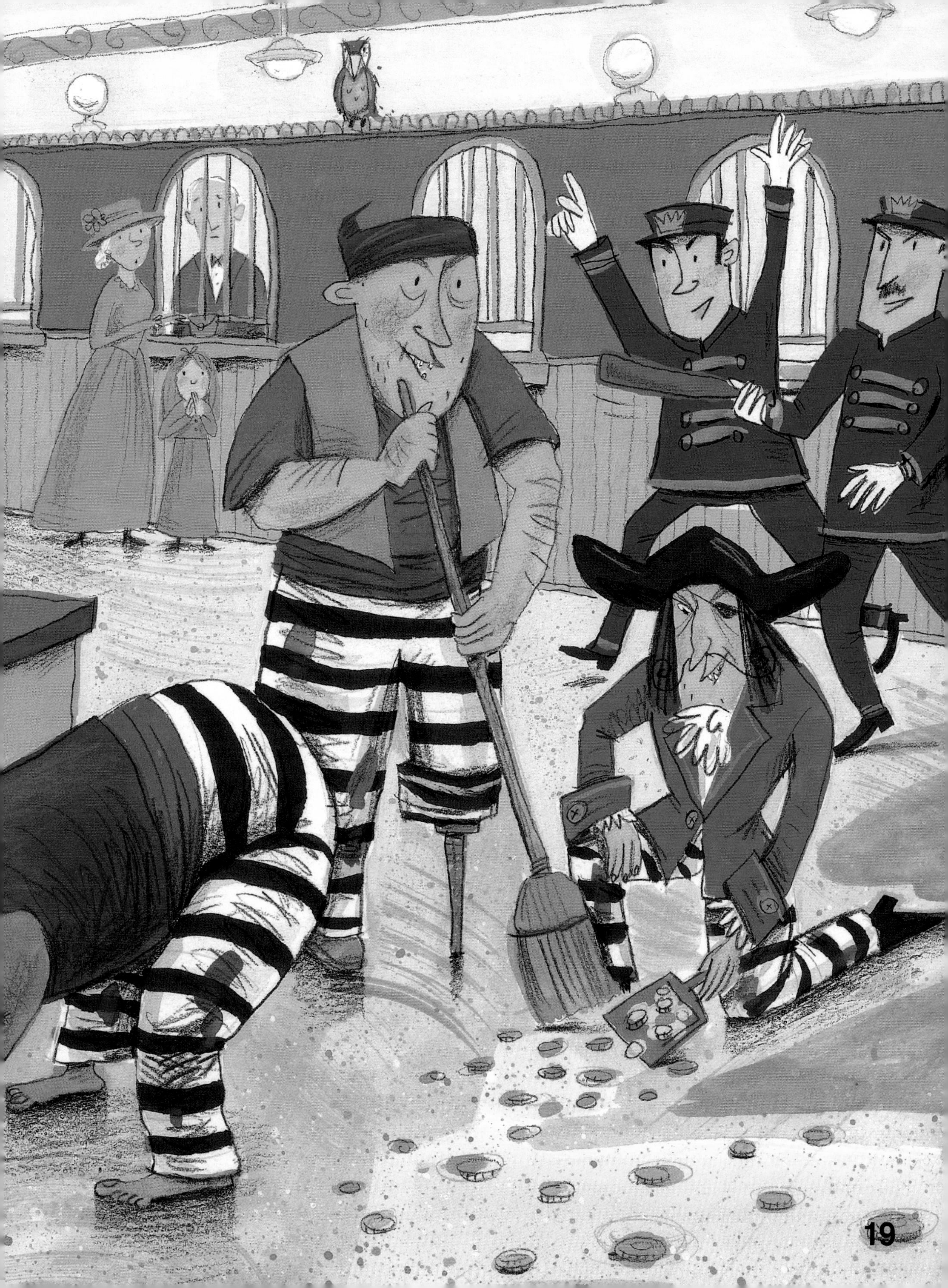

They thought it might be good to take candy from babies, so the candy wouldn't rot the babies' teeth. But the babies bit and the mothers bashed, until even Captain Squint hollered, "Mommy!"

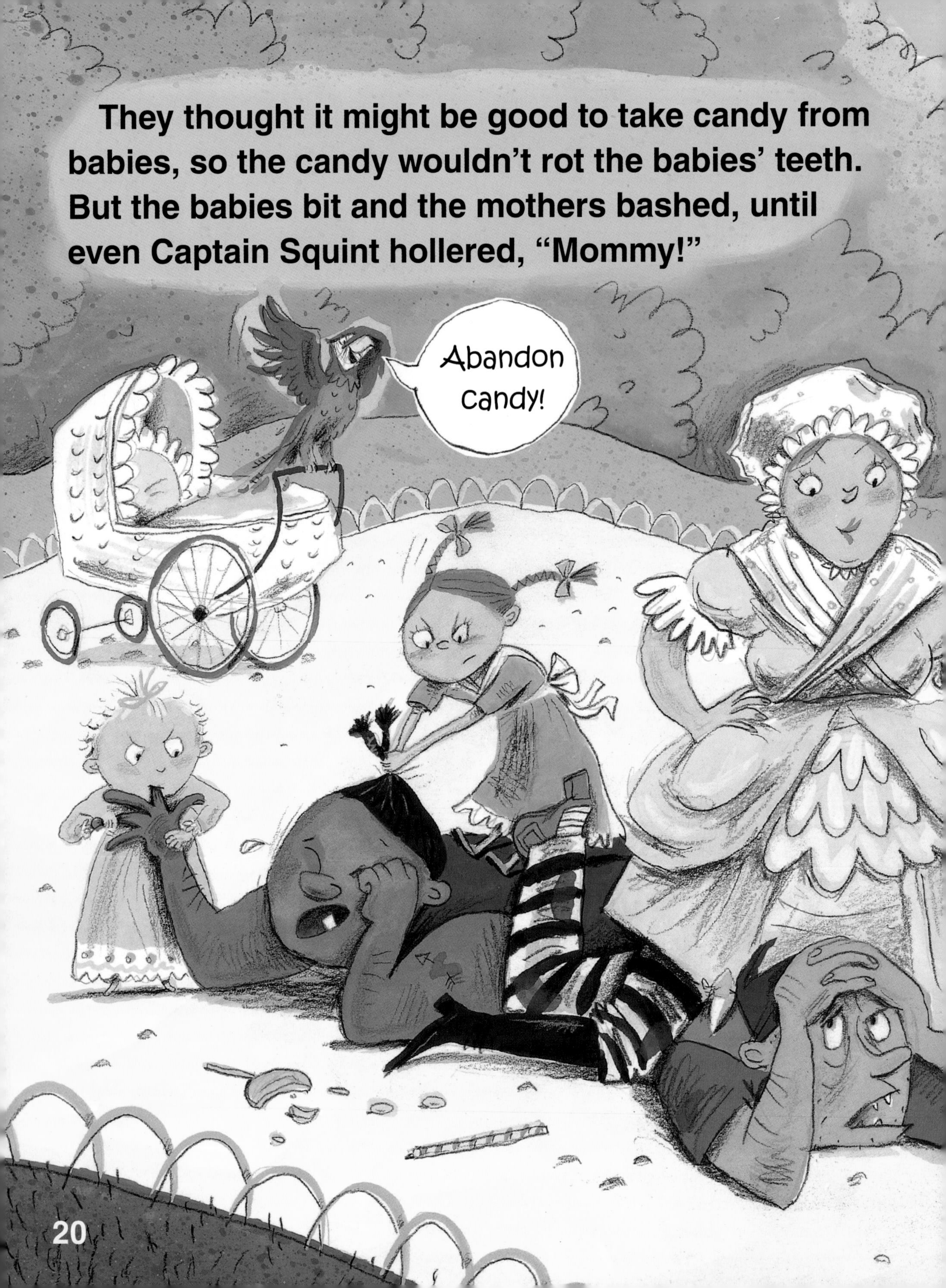
Abandon candy!

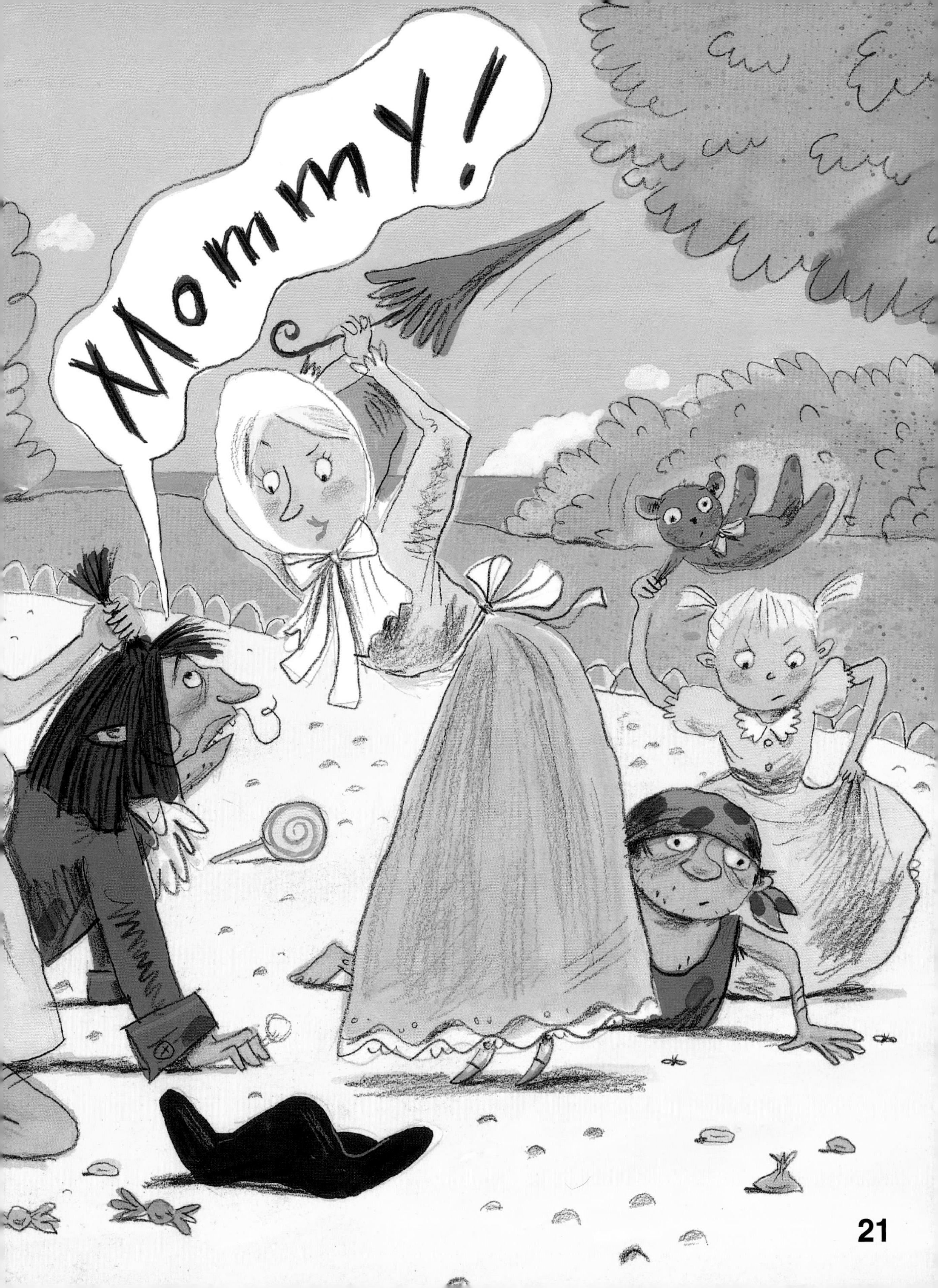
MOMMY!

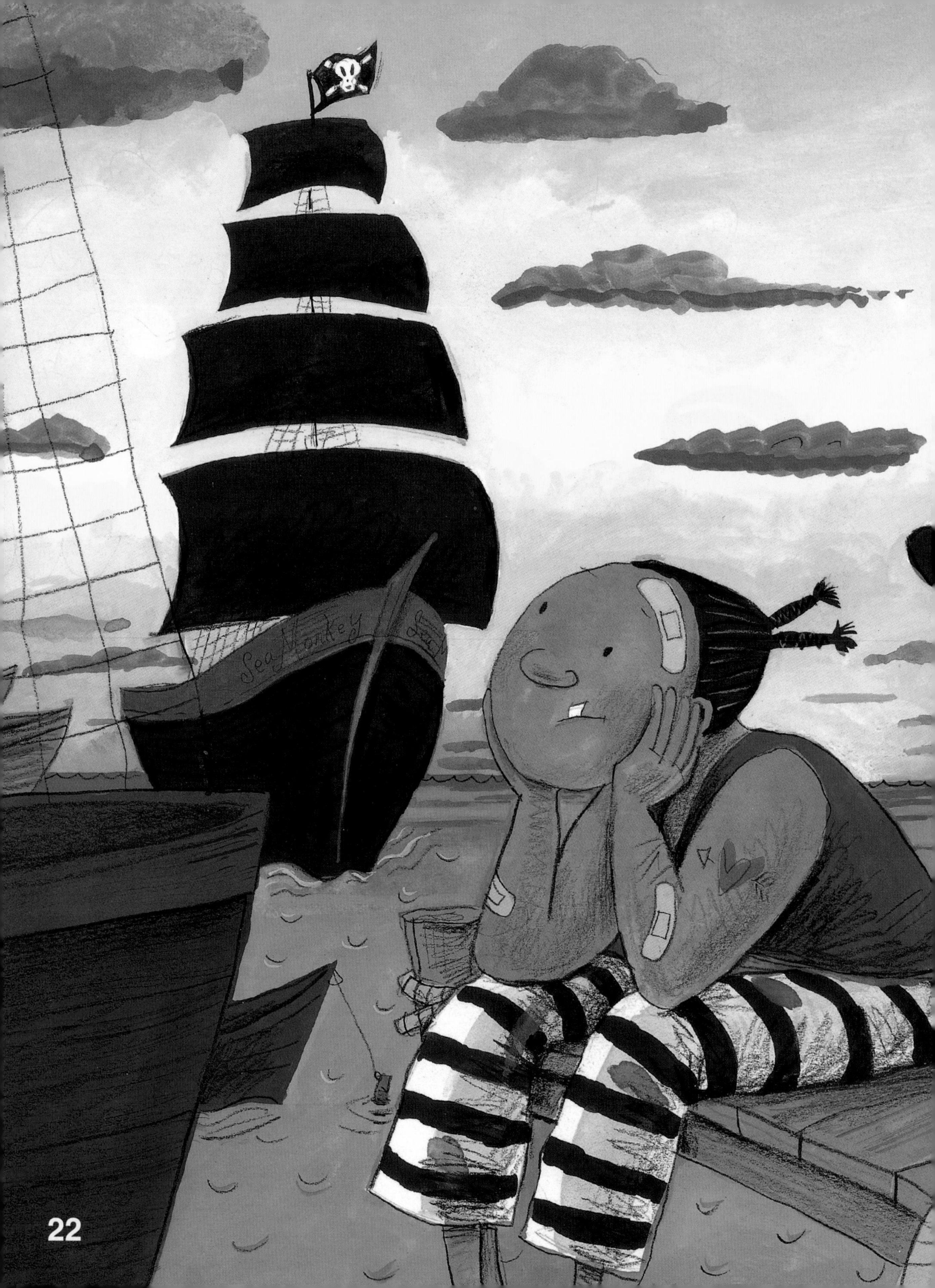
Sea Monkey

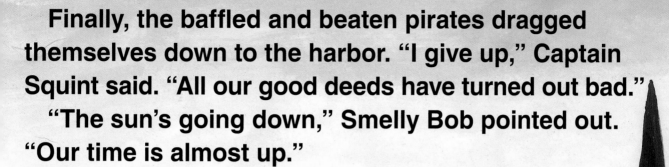

Finally, the baffled and beaten pirates dragged themselves down to the harbor. "I give up," Captain Squint said. "All our good deeds have turned out bad."

"The sun's going down," Smelly Bob pointed out. "Our time is almost up."

Just then, the notorious pirate ship Sea Monkey sailed into the harbor.

23

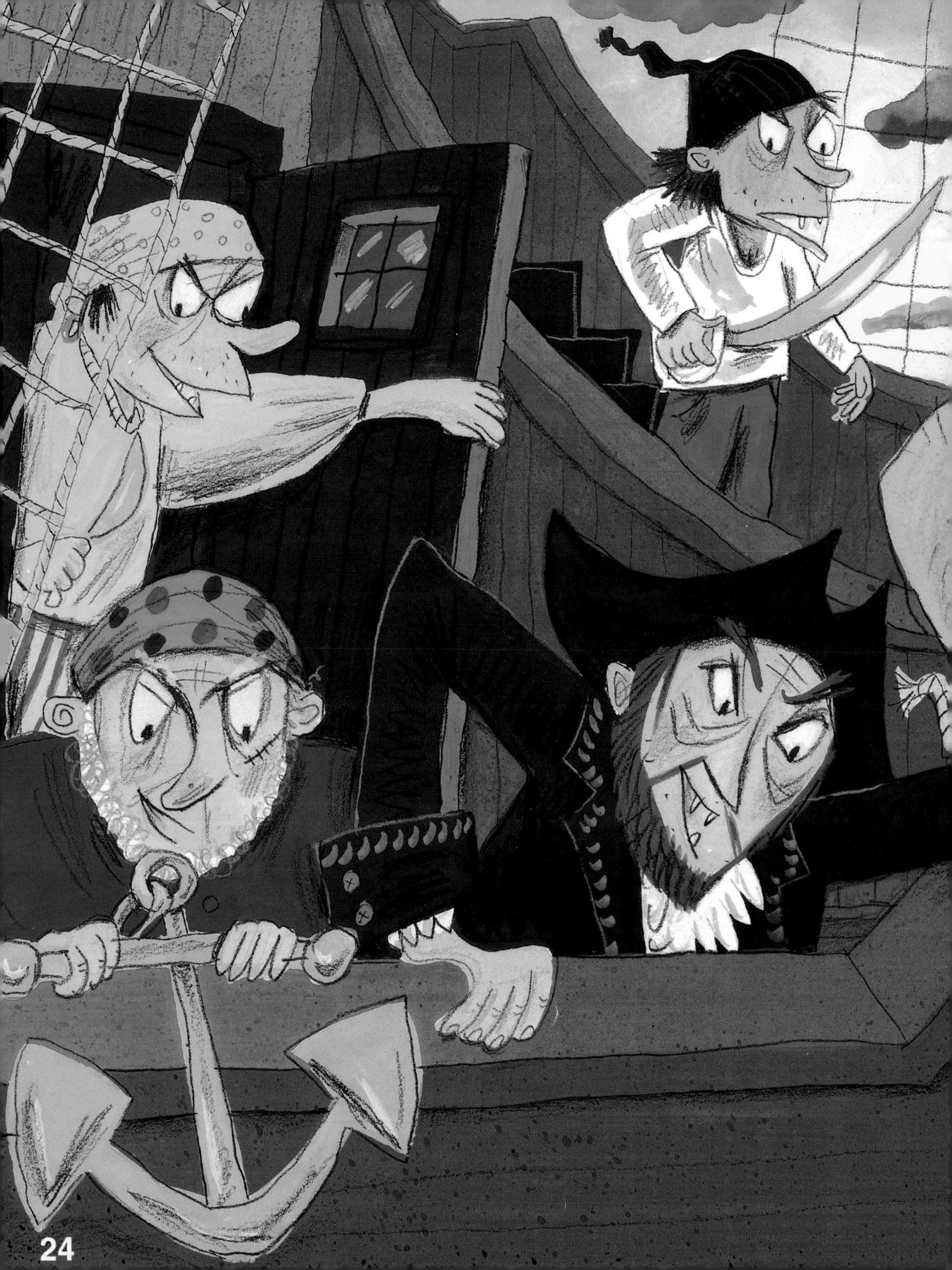

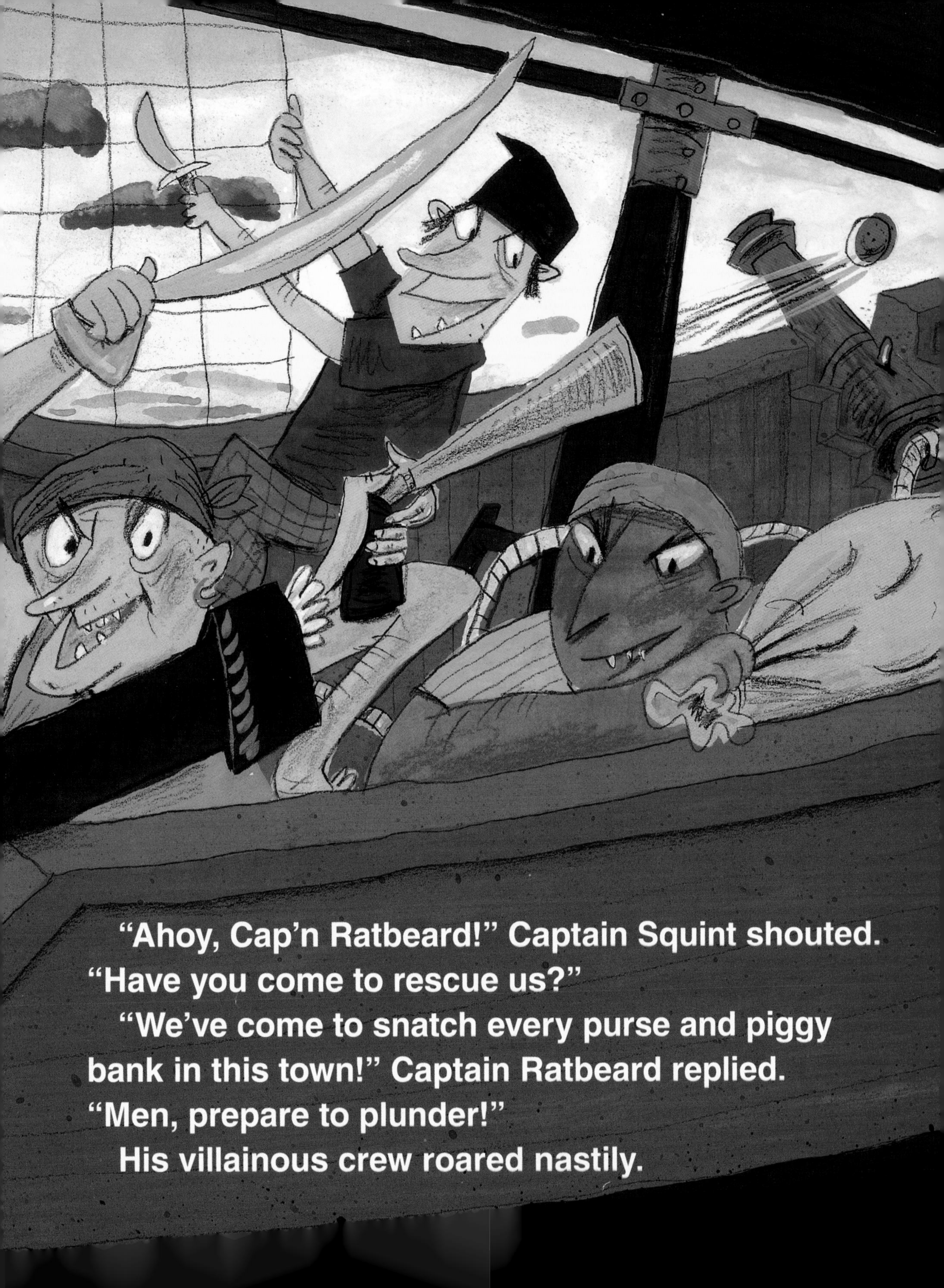

“Ahoy, Cap’n Ratbeard!” Captain Squint shouted. “Have you come to rescue us?”

“We’ve come to snatch every purse and piggy bank in this town!” Captain Ratbeard replied. “Men, prepare to plunder!”

His villainous crew roared nastily.

"Avast!" Captain Squint said. "And beware! This town is full of pirate-bashing ladies and bloodthirsty babies!"

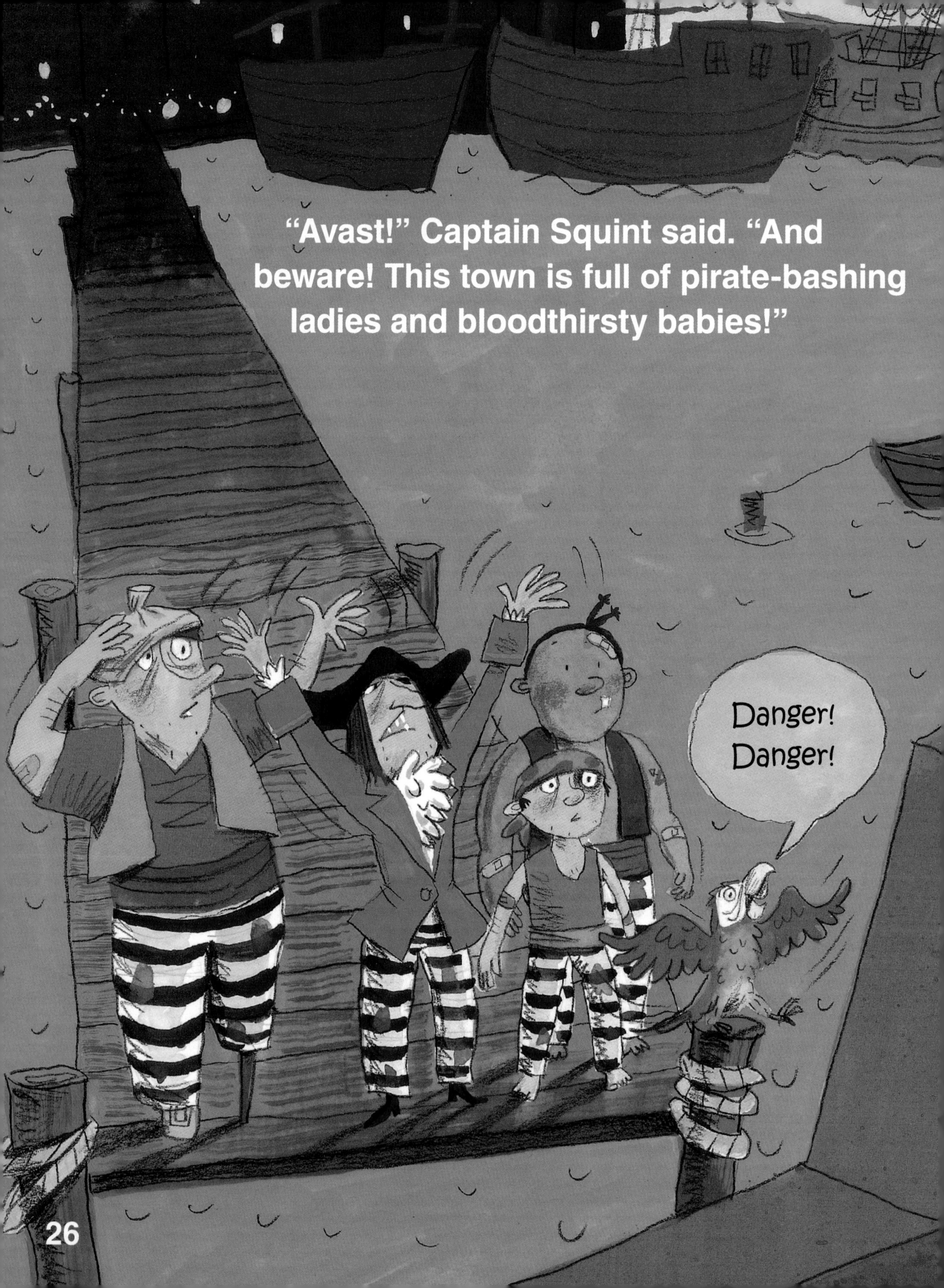
Danger!
Danger!

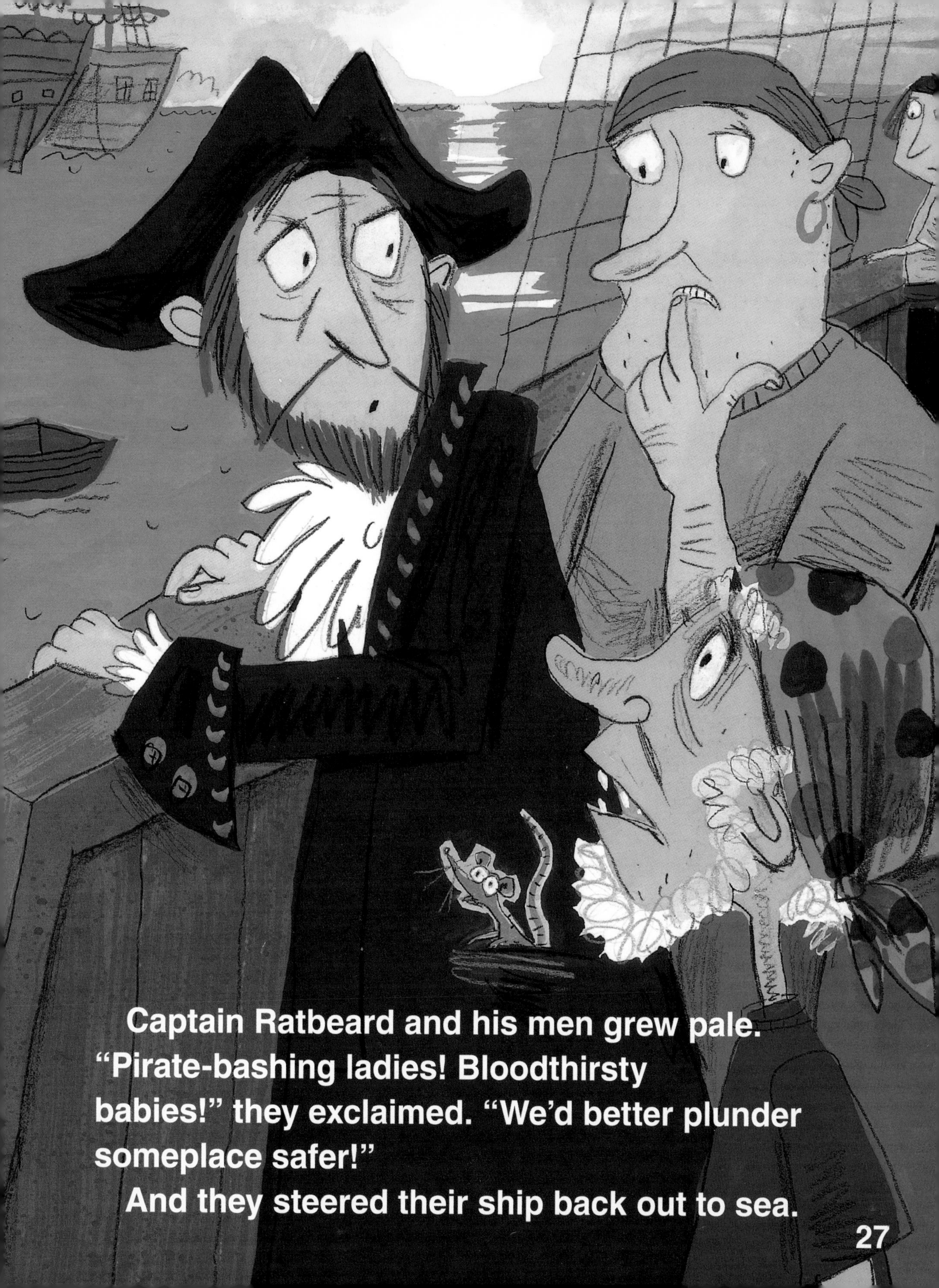

Captain Ratbeard and his men grew pale. "Pirate-bashing ladies! Bloodthirsty babies!" they exclaimed. "We'd better plunder someplace safer!"

And they steered their ship back out to sea.

As the *Sea Monkey* disappeared, a cheering crowd rushed onto the dock. “Well done!” the judge said. “You did your good deed—you saved the town!”

“We did?” Captain Squint replied.

“And you beat the deadline. So you’re free to leave.”

“We are?” said Ed the Fierce.

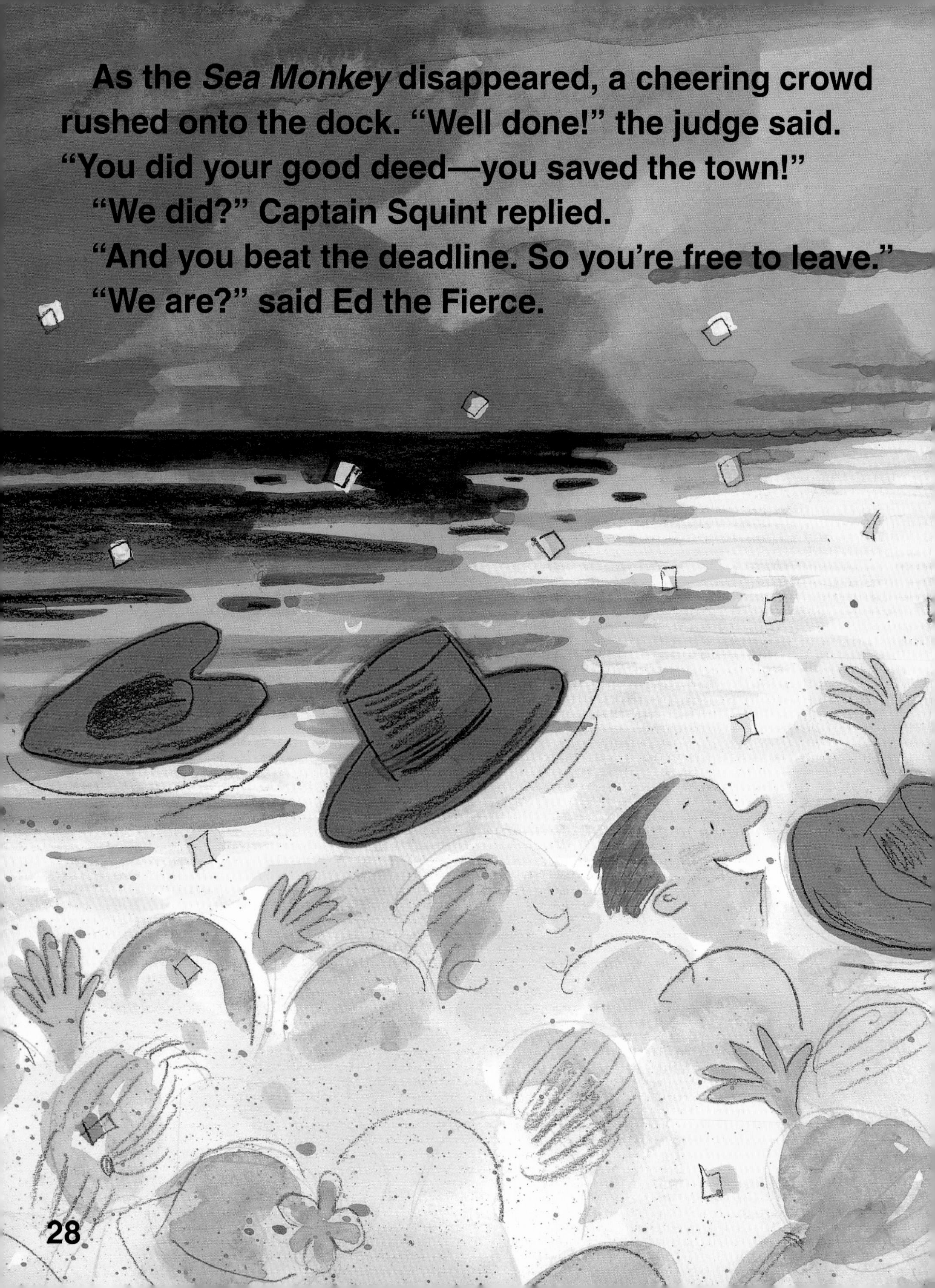

"Would you rather meet the new rats in our prison?" the judge asked.

"No thanks, matey!" the pirates cried.

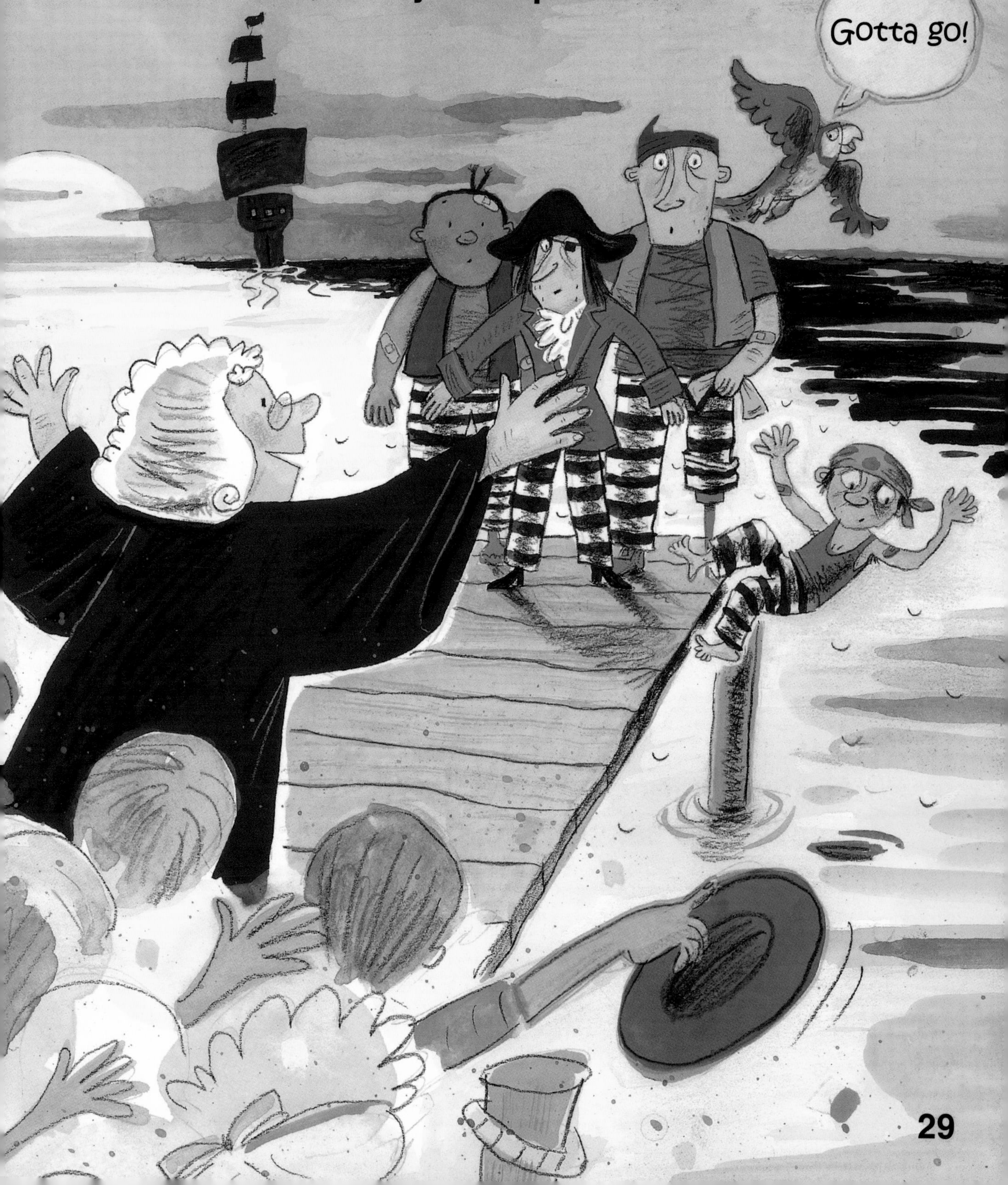
Gotta go!

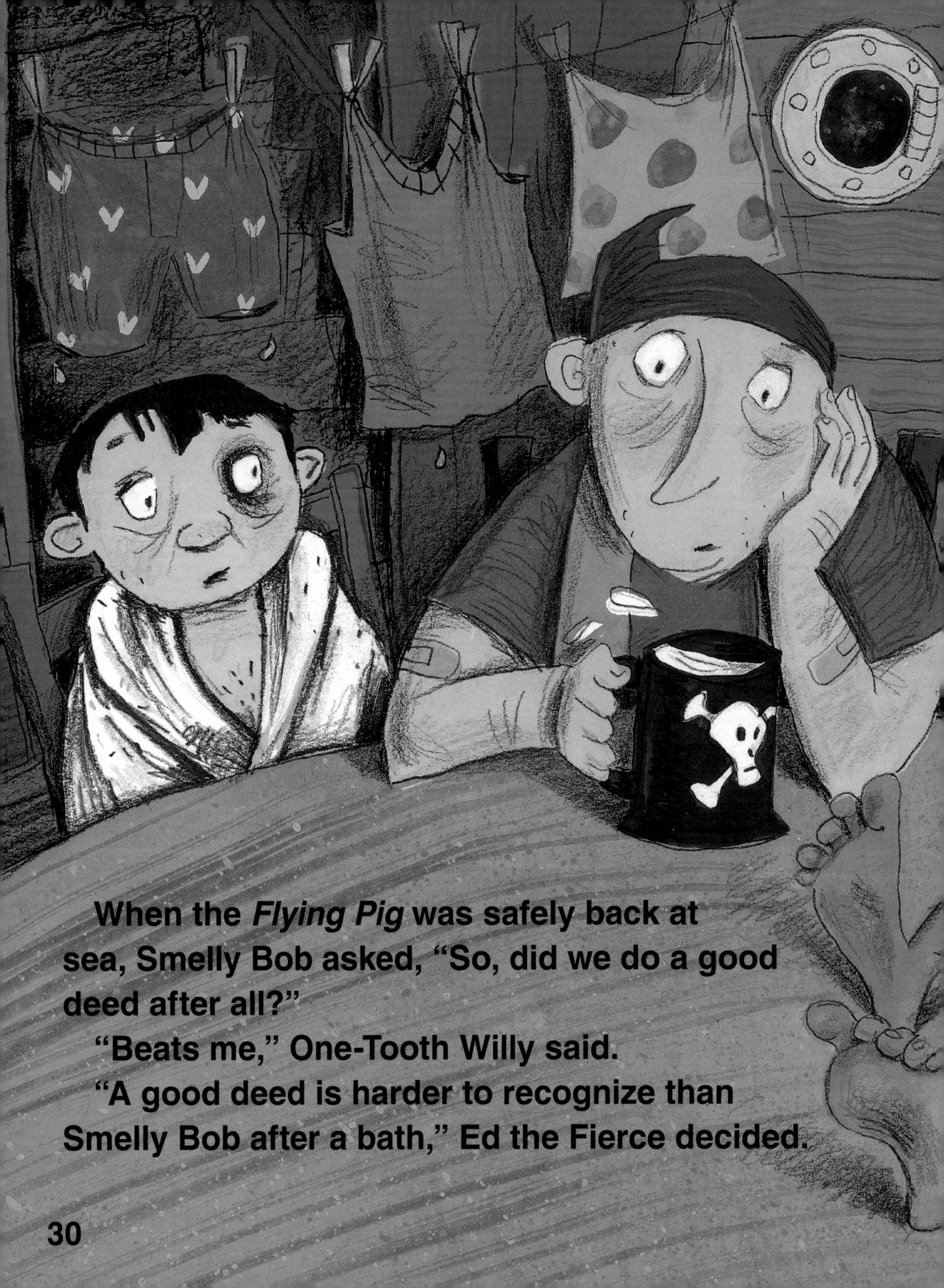

When the *Flying Pig* was safely back at sea, Smelly Bob asked, “So, did we do a good deed after all?”

“Beats me,” One-Tooth Willy said.

“A good deed is harder to recognize than Smelly Bob after a bath,” Ed the Fierce decided.

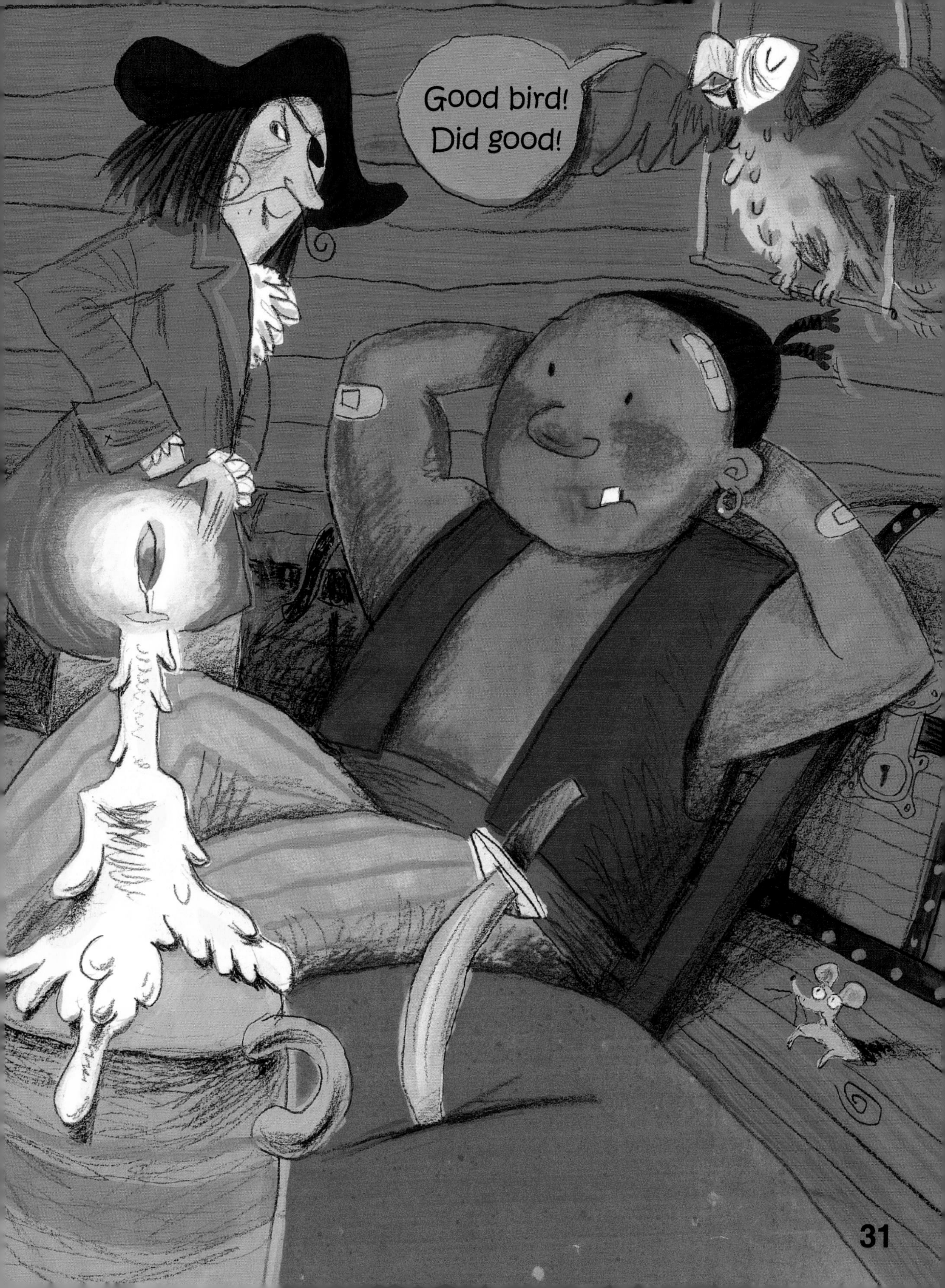
Good bird!
Did good!

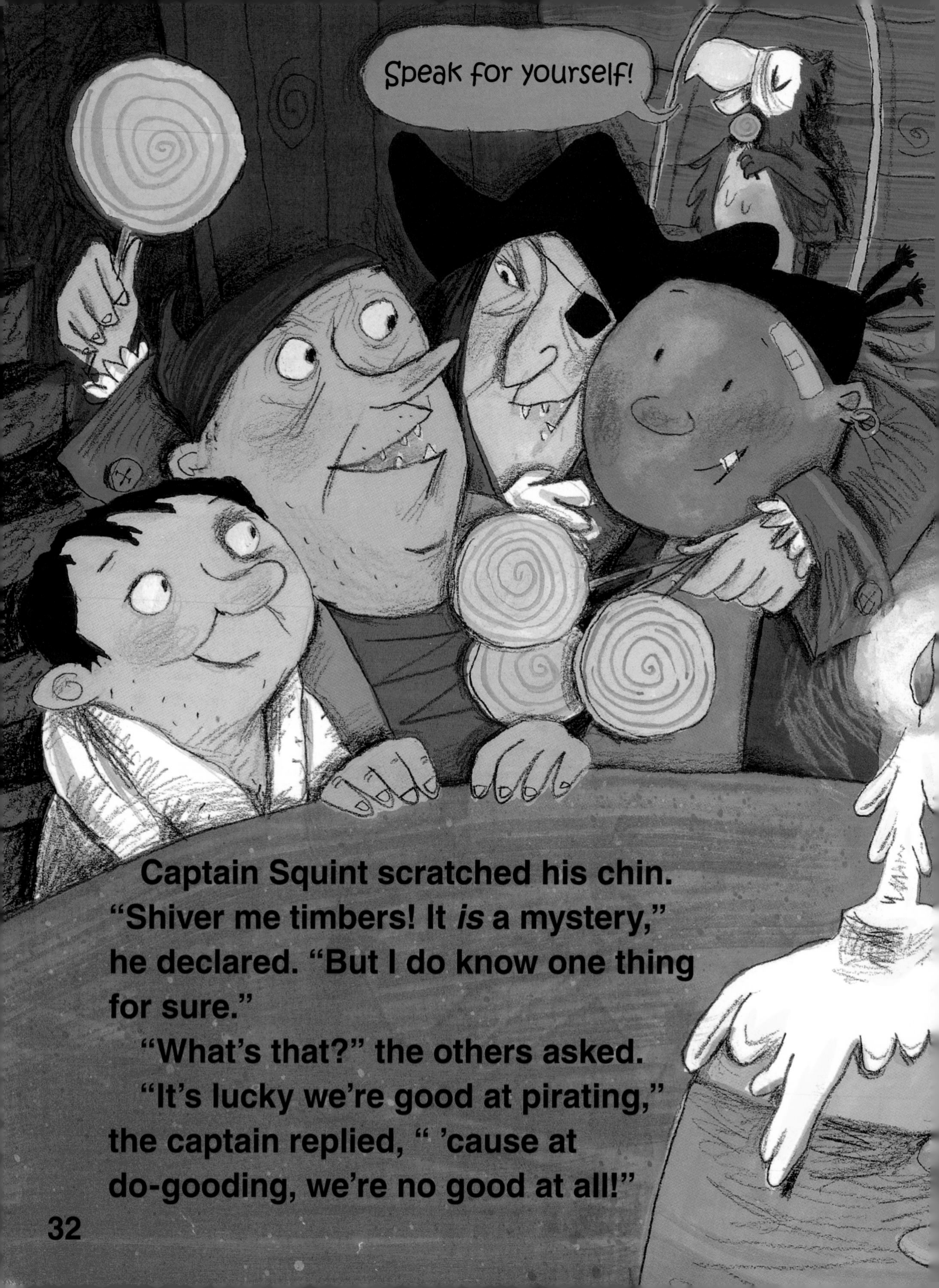
Speak for yourself!

Captain Squint scratched his chin. "Shiver me timbers! It *is* a mystery," he declared. "But I do know one thing for sure."

"What's that?" the others asked.

"It's lucky we're good at pirating," the captain replied, " 'cause at do-gooding, we're no good at all!"